Alone for Christmas: A Domestic Thriller

Foxglove Lee

Published by Rainbow Crush, 2022.

Alone for Christmas

A Domestic Thriller

Foxglove Lee

1

Marissa stared out the window, cradling a World's Best Teacher mug with both hands. She held it as though it were an injured animal, something fragile and in need of care. Her cinnamon chai was still hot, even though she'd been standing at the window for what felt like hours.

Her mind always wandered as she gazed across the backyard, watching birds land at the feeder in a vague, noncommittal way. A wandering mind could be quite freeing, or it could become a trap.

At the moment, she was in neutral. She couldn't remember what she'd been pondering moments ago. Possibly breakfast, possibly the past.

Perhaps she'd been reflecting on her final workday before winter break, when her students had piled her desk high with gingerly-wrapped Christmas presents, all of which she'd parcelled into the janitor's closet with a note that the custodial staff might keep, enjoy, or discard the gifts as suited their whims.

Home was more than just a reprieve from the hustle and bustle of the holiday season. Home was her sanctuary. Truly. She didn't know what she'd do without this space to relax in.

How on earth did she cope with Christmas when she was younger? Living first with her mother and siblings while they celebrated the season—joyfully oblivious to the crushing anxiety every ribbon and wreath and sprig of mistletoe caused her—and then with Ted, who'd been a perfectly nice guy—she wouldn't have married a jerk—but he never fully understood her aversion to all things Christmas.

Life was better with Nick.

They say second marriages tend to be more successful, and that's certainly been their experience. Nick had also been married before. His divorce had been amicable. There'd been mutual agreement that he and his first wife wed too young. No kids were involved, and so the solution seemed simple.

His separation story was a mirror to Marissa's: one of the many things that drew her to him, in the beginning. She felt understood. Plus, they were both teachers. They shared a passion for pedagogy. They worked at the same school, back then, and so she had a chance to watch him for a while and warm up to him slowly. He never came on too strong. It scared Marissa when men pursued her forcefully. She felt hunted, like an animal. Like a rabbit.

Marissa sipped her milky tea and watched house sparrows battle juncos for spots at the feeder. Snow had fallen overnight, coating her backyard in a blanket of winter white. She'd once heard a statistic saying that shopping malls were more crowded on days like today. The weather got people in the mood for Christmas. The population was willing to spend more money when it was snowing.

There were times when Marissa wished she were more like other people. Maybe she'd make more friends if she enjoyed the holidays. Other teachers gave her gifts around Christmastime, and she presented them with nothing. It didn't take long before the rumour mill began its familiar churn. By mid-January, every kindling friendship disintegrated into cold looks and persistent snubs. Her coworkers took her for an icy-hearted snob.

If only people could magically understand without the need for her to explain. Marissa didn't want to tell the world the true extent of her trauma, and she shouldn't have to.

Why couldn't others give her the benefit of the doubt?

Nick tried to persuade Marissa not to describe herself as damaged goods, but she took a certain comfort in seeing herself that way. She would never be like other people, whether she wished to or not.

She would never enjoy the holiday season.

Though they'd been married for more than three years, Nick and Marissa had never spent Christmas together. Long before they met, Nick had become involved with a volunteer organization that builds latrines in various countries around the world. He didn't provide his services for the accolades, nor yet for the money, since the work didn't pay. It was just one of the many tasks he took on throughout the year for the improvement of humanity.

He was a good man, her husband.

This particular jaunt coincided with the winter school holiday, meaning Nick spent every Christmas far from home, leaving Marissa all alone.

No tree to decorate, no presents to wrap, no stockings to fill, no turkey to roast.

In short, no Christmas.

She couldn't have planned it better herself.

If Nick spent the holidays at home, Marissa would be expected to mark the occasion in some small way. Nick was not exactly a Christmas enthusiast himself—his first wife had been a collector of seasonal knickknacks to the extent that he classified her as a holiday hoarder—but he would probably opt for a small tree and a modest turkey and, at very least, a gift exchange.

When she told him how triggering the trappings of Christmas were for her, he said he understood, but how could he? Nobody else did. Even her own family didn't get it, and they knew all the gritty details. Nick had a vague notion of what happened to her as a child, but he could never fully grasp the true terror she lived with, even now.

All these years later.

The shrill scream of a blue jay caused every sparrow in the yard to flee. The cascade of birds brought Marissa back to the present moment. She watched them scatter to the leafless trees at the back of the yard while the solitary jay took up residence at the feeder.

In the summertime, the yard felt lovely and private. Marissa spent much of her time out there, devouring novel after novel, drinking orange juice mixed with sparkling water. Sometimes she accompanied Nick to his volunteer sessions, but mostly she stayed home. She felt safe in the backyard. When the trees were lush with greenery, you'd think you were alone in the world.

Not so, during the winter months. Once the leaves fell, Marissa became amply aware of the townhouses built practically at the foot of her yard. They'd been there before she and Nick moved in, so they were nothing new, but she did somewhat resent their proximity.

Even now, as she watched the birds cluster in the naked trees, she could see Mrs. Jones in the house across the way. Marissa's birdwatching window looked right into the widow's kitchen, where she stood contemplatively over the stove, stirring a large pot of something-or-other.

Soup, most likely.

Nick was more chummy with the neighbours, and he'd reported to Marissa that, ever since Mr. Jones's death in February, Mrs. Jones had been filling her hours with community service. Preparing meals for those less fortunate—that was her main focus. She'd always enjoyed cooking for her husband. Now that he was gone, it helped her to fill the hours feeding the hungry. Nick admired the woman greatly. She was active for her age, a pillar of the community.

Circling her fingers along the underside of her mug, Marissa contemplated the woman's kindly expression. Two lonely ladies separated by two panes of glass and a stretch of yard. That was them.

Marissa ought to pay Mrs. Jones a visit after Christmas, just to be neighbourly.

That's what Nick would do, if he were around.

As if in response to Marissa's thought, Mrs. Jones began laughing, then turned to address someone else in the kitchen. A man. Marissa couldn't see him, but she could tell from the way the woman's eyes crinkled.

For a moment, Marissa felt a sense of shock. How dare Mrs. Jones become involved with someone else so fast? Within a year of her husband's death! It was unseemly. But, then, how long after Marissa was separated did she start seeing Nick? Only a matter of months, she'd say. Anyway, it was no crime—a widow taking up with someone who was no doubt kind and lonely, like herself. All the best to that pair.

Marissa felt like somewhat of a Peeping Tom now that she knew Mrs. Jones had company, so she turned her attention away from the window. Not easy to stay entertained, this time of year, if you were avoiding Christmas. She couldn't turn on the radio, because that was all holiday tunes. She couldn't turn on the TV because of the glut of corny Christmas movies.

The holidays were everywhere, except inside Marissa's house.

She read for a while, dozing on and off throughout the afternoon. Streaming content seemed a safe way to go, but she couldn't find anything that interested her particularly.

Her mind began to wander in directions it ought not go.

Though it was early in the evening when she decided to go to bed, consciousness weighed too heavily upon her. She took a pill and let it guide her graciously into sleep.

2

It was not yet morning when Marissa awoke.

On high alert.

Why?

She'd taken a sleeping pill. She didn't usually wake up this way when she'd taken one. When she hadn't taken one, yes, but with this drug in her system? No.

The whole world buzzed around her. She could hear the air. She could see nothing but the digital clock citing 3:55. In all her life, had she ever been awake at this hour? Not in recent memory, that's for sure.

A thud from the attic. That's why she'd tunnelled so sharply out of sleep. A thud from above.

There it was again. No, not a thud this time. A footstep. A creak.

Was she dreaming? Another nightmare? How could she know for sure whether she was asleep or awake? Her mind seemed sharp as a blade, but her body dared not move. Was fear keeping her in place, or was this the effect of medication? How could she say for certain?

Who was in her house? How had they entered inside? Why were they in the attic?

Marissa's heart pounded. For a moment, she could hear nothing but the pulsing of her own blood. She begged her body to relax, otherwise how could she tell what was going on above her?

There. Another shuffle. Not a footstep, but a shifting noise.

The attic was storage space. Nothing worth any money up there. Only Nick's sentimental items, childhood memories he'd reclaimed when his parents died.

Why would a cat burglar be up there?

No, a cat burglar would rifle through the jewellery box, and the jewellery box was in the bedroom with Marissa. She'd locked herself in, as she did whenever she was home alone, but if someone really wanted to get in they could probably kick down the door.

Was Marissa safer inside or out?

If she made a run for it, would the burglar chase her downstairs and nab her before she got free? Would she do better to stay put, make not a sound, pretend as though the house were empty until the intruder had gone?

If he'd come for her, he'd have come to her directly.

Anyway, the question was moot. She couldn't move. She'd tried and tried. She could scarcely wiggle her toes, let alone dart for the door. She couldn't roll over in bed.

She couldn't even turn her head.

Frozen in place, she listened with acute precision for the next shuffle, the next scrape of boots on a dusty floor. Even the tiniest noise from above rang in her ears like microphone feedback through a wall of amplifiers. Her muscles grew so tight she felt locked in her bed, locked inside her own body.

Had life not tormented her enough?

What had she done to deserve this ordeal?

Another sound, now, as though a body were being dragged across the floor. What on earth was happening in her attic?

Perhaps she was wrong, though. She couldn't always trust her own perceptions. Trauma had strange effects on the body and the brain. Those like Marissa, who'd been affected early in life, could never fully trust their own senses. What she was interpreting as a resonant thud could be no more than a soft thump. She couldn't be certain of anything she heard.

She couldn't even be sure she was awake.

Yes, she was. She was. This was no dream. She knew the difference. Someone was moving across the attic, to the trapdoor, down the stairs. Moving quickly, now. So fast the intruder's footfalls kept pace with Marissa's racing heart. Rapid pace, heart-race. She held her breath, all the better to hear this man as he ran.

What was this, now? Shutting the trap? Thoughtful robber. Did he think he could escape unnoticed? And she'd never know he'd been in her house? She'd never know what he stole?

He came across the hallway, ever closer to the room where she lay locked away yet powerless to move. As he approached the bedroom, she started a chant, like a wish or a prayer, just inside her own head:

Please go.

Please leave.

Don't find me.

Just go.

Please go.

Please leave.

Don't find me.

Just go.

But he stopped outside her doorway. She could hear nothing. No footsteps. No movement, but no silence, either. Just the sound of another person inside her house. The breath of another. The heightened sense of awareness.

Someone was there. On the other side of that door. Someone was there.

And then he wasn't. He was gone, taking the stairs at a jog. Out the door. She heard it.

Open and shut.

He had come and he had gone.

What had he taken?

Marissa's sense of security, for a start.

What else?

Who's to know? She couldn't move a muscle, not even to reach for her phone.

3

T ime crawled.

Marissa could neither move nor sleep as she watched the clock. How could a minute last such a long time? She counted to sixty, but always too fast. No matter how she tried to slow her count, she could never slow it enough to fall in time with the clock.

She wouldn't call the police. Bad enough she'd had one intruder in her house. She didn't want strange men poking around her place, asking why she hadn't run, why she hadn't called earlier. Maybe, they'd suggest, this was one of those insurance scams where the householders stash their precious possessions at a friend's place and then pretend they've been burgled.

Marissa wanted protection. That's not what police provided.

Nearly an hour went by before Marissa was able to move. She inched up the bed until she was moderately inclined. Then, at long last, she reached for her phone.

She couldn't call Nick. He always turned his phone off when he left the country. Roaming charges were far too steep. He might be able to pick up an email at some point, but what would she tell him? To come home right away? No, he was doing so much good where he was. He ought to stay with his volunteer group.

Though she didn't hold out much hope, Marissa opened up her contacts. The first name on that list was Asim, a colleague from the school she'd worked at two years back. Most teachers didn't make it into her contacts list, but she'd taken a shine to Asim. She always felt more comfortable around gay men than straight ones, and one time Marissa overheard him admonishing two other teachers who were badmouthing her in front of a student. From then on, he was golden.

Asim lived only a few blocks away. She knew because she'd picked up his mail one summer, when he and his boyfriend were out of town. She and Asim weren't exactly bosom buddies, but he was the closest Marissa had to a friend—apart from her husband, of course. Nick and Marissa were friends above all. She trusted him, and she didn't trust many people. Men, in particular.

The men she did trust, she trusted with her life.

Marissa put her phone on the night table.

A wintery dawn broke silently through the curtains. The blue-grey light gave her a certain amount of hope—hope, at least, that she could rise from her bed and investigate. If it had snowed overnight, there would be shoe prints on the front walk.

Although, what good would shoe prints be if she didn't call the cops?

And even if it had snowed, well, her neighbour to the right thought he was being chivalrous by keeping her walkway cleared while Nick was away. She didn't trust the guy. She thought he just liked creeping close to her house so he had an excuse to peek in the front window.

Marissa's stomach knotted as she slipped out of bed. The air felt unusually cold. She always turned down the heat overnight, but even so...

Grabbing the chenille throw from the end of the bed, she wrapped it around her shoulders and peeked outside. No new snow that she could see. The only light in any of the townhouse windows belonged to Mrs. Jones. Even at this early hour, her kitchen glowed like a hurricane lamp. She was probably up early to get a jump start on her soup-stirring duties.

Clutching her abdomen, Marissa moved toward the bedroom door. She didn't want to look in the hall, but she knew she would have to, eventually.

Or maybe she could just stay in her bedroom for the rest of the day.

Maybe she could stay there for the rest of her life.

She knew nobody was in her house. No one but herself. Even so, she pressed her ear to the door, straining to listen. She heard nothing, of course. What was there to hear?

In that moment, a banging noise shook the entire house. Marissa bolted from the door. Her heart pounded so hard she thought it would burst from her chest to hit the wall with a bloody thump.

As she stood by her bedside, clinging to the carved oak post, her whole body trembled. Marissa had experienced a lot of fear in her life—more than any human deserved to feel—but the past few hours had been supernaturally terrorizing.

After a moment, when the ringing in her ears faded to a tinny whisper, she realized the heat had come on. That explained the banging noise. It was nothing to be afraid of. Just normal house noises, the same ones she heard every day of her life. Her terror had caused her to overreact, to think it was something more than it was. That's all. No threat. No explosion. No nothing. Just heat.

If she hadn't felt so tense, she'd have laughed at herself.

Even though she knew nothing was amiss and it was only the heating system that had scared her, Marissa still felt as though something were dreadfully wrong.

Well, her house had been broken into at four in the morning. There'd been someone in the attic. There was that.

She knew she'd locked the door before she went to bed. She always checked the locks. So she felt she could be forgiven for acting a little jumpy on this particular morning.

Marissa crept toward the bedroom door slowly, until she was only inches away. She took hold of the doorknob, but didn't turn it. She simply stood there, watching the door, wishing it were a window, or maybe that two-way glass they had at police stations. If only she could see through it without any danger of being spotted herself.

It took a matter of minutes before she'd worked up the mental strength to open that door, and when she did it was only a crack. Just enough to glance into the hall.

What she saw there tore a scream from her throat.

She slammed the door and locked it before leaping across the room and onto her bed. What good would blankets do? And yet she felt safer beneath them, phone in hand.

Any other day, at any other moment, she'd worry what a man like him might think of her—that she was crazy, no doubt—but on this day and in this moment, she shamelessly called the first contact on her list. With Nick out of town, he was the only person she could trust.

"Asim?" she said the moment he picked up. Without waiting for a reply, she cried, "He's been inside my house, Asim. There's tinsel on the floor. It's not possible. I know he's dead, but I'm sure he was here."

4

Marissa perched at the front window like a loyal hound as she awaited Asim's arrival. When she spotted him turning the corner onto her street, she rushed to the door. Yanking it open, she raced all the way to the sidewalk before realizing she didn't have socks on her feet, much less shoes. Winter's cold shattered her body.

She waved to Asim, then fled back inside.

After being out in the frigid morning air, home felt practically tropical. Her feet blazed, and her toes glowed red. She shouldn't have gone outside with no shoes on, but she hadn't been thinking. As soon as she saw Asim, she felt she had to get to him immediately or else something horrible would happen.

"Knock knock," he said, since she hadn't closed the door behind her.

"You're here," she cried, throwing herself at him—an uncharacteristic move, for her.

Asim gave a reluctant chuckle as Marissa wrapped her arms around his puffy red jacket. "What's wrong?" he asked. "You sounded panic-stricken on the phone, but I couldn't understand a word of it. Someone broke in? Or died?"

"I'm so sorry," she said, tugging him into her house by his jacket pockets. "I'm sure you've got better things to do, but I didn't know who else to call."

"It's fine. Don't worry about that. I'm glad you reached out—hey, let's get this door closed before we let Old Man Winter in, okay?"

Marissa released her hold on Asim's pockets, but wrapped both hands around his wrist. She knew she was acting like a child, but now that her protector was here, she wouldn't let him out of her grasp.

Once the door was closed, Asim asked, "What's going on, Riss? I've never seen you like this."

"I'm sorry," she repeated. "I don't want to be a nuisance, only something happened last night—or this morning, I guess—that scared me out of my mind. I needed to talk to someone I can trust."

Asim's expression of concern softened into sympathy. "You can trust me, Riss. You know that, I hope."

She nodded so violently her brain felt like it was bouncing around inside her skull.

When she burst into tears, he hesitated, then hugged her. She was glad he did. It's exactly what she needed in that moment: to feel safe and secure in a strong man's arms. And Asim was one of the strongest men she knew. He would probably be at the gym right now, if he hadn't taken her call. The guy was all muscle and masculinity, but there was a softness to his personality that made him infinitely appealing, especially at a time like this.

"Hey, hey, hey—let's sit you down," Asim said, guiding Marissa into the front room.

When he shrugged away from her, she cried out, "Don't leave me!" and felt instantly ashamed of herself. "I'm sorry. I shouldn't have said that. You're allowed to leave, if you want to."

"No need to be sorry," he calmly replied. "I'm not going anywhere. I'm just taking off my coat, if that's okay."

She sniffed and wiped her face with the sleeve of her pyjama top. "Yes, that's fine. Oh, I'm a terrible hostess. I should have offered you coffee or tea or—"

"You don't need to offer me anything," Asim assured her. "Just sit yourself down. You're trembling."

She slumped onto the couch, pulling the chenille throw tight around her body as Asim draped his jacket across the far side of the couch. He must have come here straight out of bed. All he had on was a pair of grey track pants and a blue v-neck tee that had been worn so often it was nearly translucent. Even though it wasn't quite skin-tight, his spectacular muscles glowed easily through.

When he joined her on the couch, she threw her arms around him and pressed her cheek to his chest. "I'm sorry I'm doing this."

"It's fine," he told her, resting his hand gently on her back. "I'm here for you, Riss. Just tell me what you need."

5

Did her story even make sense?

The way she told it, with her words all running together, she wasn't sure anyone could have figured out what she was trying to say.

Asim didn't seem to understand why tinsel would scare a person as much as it scared her. She tried to explain that it wasn't the tinsel itself that was inherently frightening. Any signifier of Christmastime would have freaked her out just as much. It wouldn't have mattered whether a glass ornament or silver bell or gingerbread man had been left outside her bedroom door. Anything along those lines would have scared her out of her mind.

She *was* going out of her mind, wasn't she? Clearly, she was. Asim could be honest with her. Her feelings wouldn't be hurt.

"I don't think you're crazy," he assured her, holding her close.

She loved the smell of him, of man things and sleep.

"But if someone broke into your house, it's really a police matter."

"No!" Marissa cried.

She looked him plain in the face, and he could obviously see that she was serious, because he calmly said, "Okay. No police. I get it."

Fighting back tears, she said, "No you don't."

"Maybe if you explained..." He stopped himself and revised. "But you don't have to. You can tell me what you're comfortable saying, but if it's too private or too painful, I understand."

When she didn't say anything, he asked, "Is Nick... does he... hurt you?"

"No!" Marissa found herself laughing. The idea was so ludicrous. "This has nothing to do with my husband."

"Your ex, then?"

"Nothing to do with him, either. Ted was always good to me. And Nick is one of the best men I know. He's so generous and thoughtful. He would never do anything to hurt me. Same goes for Ted."

"Don't get mad," Asim began. "But you're sure someone was in the house? It wasn't a dream?"

"It couldn't have been a dream," Marissa pleaded. "The tinsel!"

"I know, but mice, sometimes... I mean, you heard something in the attic. Mice love attics. And a piece of tinsel is easy enough for a rodent to bring downstairs. They can move through the walls, you know."

Marissa shuddered. "We don't have mice."

He'd told her not to get mad, but she was mad. She felt furious that her only friend didn't believe her.

"There was someone in my house," she growled. "Whether or not you think it's true, he was here."

"Okay," Asim replied. "You're right. I'm sorry. I shouldn't have... you're right."

Marissa's shoulders fell. The apology worked wonders, and now she felt like a pitiable mess.

"Asim?" she squeaked. Holding back tears, she asked him, "Do you believe in ghosts?"

His body tensed. "I don't know. You think a ghost broke in?"

"Don't make fun of me," she pleaded.

"I won't," he said. "I'm not. Only..."

"It's hard to believe, I know," she interrupted. "And I'm not even sure it was him. It could have been someone else—someone living—trying to scare me. But what if it *was* him? What if he's tormenting me from beyond the grave?"

Shaking his head, Asim asked, "Who are we talking about, here?"

Was she really going to tell him? She couldn't look at him and say.

Using the chenille throw as a veil, she hid her face before recounting the events that had shattered her life. Not in detail, of course. She couldn't bear to say those words. She couldn't bear to say his name.

"Now you see why Christmas is impossible?" she pleaded. "That's when the family gathered each year. That's when we were all in one house. And I was a sickly kid to begin with. All the others would go out carolling, or take a trip to the Christmas market, or the puppet show at the library, and I wouldn't feel well enough to go sometimes. He'd be the first one volunteering to stay home and look after me."

Asim took a sharp breath.

"I would beg my mother not to go, but he would tell her she ought to enjoy the holidays with the others. So she'd go, and leave me alone with him, the house smelling like cinnamon and cloves, mistletoe over the door, the stockings all hung. Everything about this time of year takes me back to those days. I'll never get to enjoy Christmas, Asim. He took that from me. He took everything."

Asim's response was good. He said what she wanted to hear, which was, "I'm sorry you went through all that. I'm here for you—whatever you need."

He held her tight while she hid inside her chenille blanket. He didn't try to take it off, or encourage her to come out. He let her remain as hidden as she wished, and that's exactly what she needed.

After a while he asked, "So, you think that's who came to your house last night?"

"Even though he's dead?" Marissa laughed wryly at herself. "I know it sounds crazy. I probably am crazy, thinking a ghost is trying to torture me. But if someone was bad in life, wouldn't they be bad in death? Why would they change into a good person once they're gone?"

When Asim didn't say anything, Marissa pulled the blanket from over her head. She told him, "People used to comfort me by saying he's in hell now, but I don't think I believe in heaven and hell. I don't know what I believe in, some days."

Asim stared into nothingness for a strangely long time before asking, "Have you ever heard of the jinn?"

6

"Jinn?" Marissa asked. "Is that the same as a genie, like in Aladdin?"

Asim issued a sharp laugh. "Like that, yeah, except the exact opposite."

Marissa felt her cheeks glowing red, but her face was so bloated from crying Asim probably wouldn't know the difference.

"I'm not exactly an expert in Islamic lore—my parents were never very religious—but I remember my mother talking about the jinn when I was a child. The jinn are like... I guess you'd call them demons, maybe? It's said that Allah created humans, angels, and jinn. The jinn can see us, but we can't see them."

"Are they evil?" Marissa asked.

"I don't know. Probably. As I say, I'm not an expert in this stuff, but they can cause mayhem for us humans, if they want to."

"Why would they want to?"

"I don't know." Grimacing, Asim said, "I don't even know why I brought them up. When you asked about ghosts, that's what came to mind. Because ghosts... I don't know much about them, but I don't think they can move physical objects, can they?"

Marissa didn't know, either.

"But the jinn can," Asim went on. "They can manipulate your environment. They can mimic living people, or dead ones. They can tap into your deepest fears and most awful memories just to terrorize you."

"Jinn can do all that?" Marissa asked.

Asim offered half a shrug. "That's the lore. I'm no expert."

Marissa stared across the room, same thing Asim had done earlier. She jumped when her protector slapped his hands against his thighs and rose from the couch. "First things first: I'm going up to the attic to make sure nobody's there. If an actual human broke into your house, there's no way I'm leaving you alone in this place."

She hoped he wouldn't leave her alone even if something inhuman had broken in, but she didn't say so. Instead, she said, "I heard him leave. Person, ghost, jinn—whatever he was, he came down the attic stairs, down the main stairs, then out the door."

"This door?" Asim asked, stepping into the front hall.

Marissa nodded, following him as he opened the door and flipped the lock a few times.

"Let me ask you this," Asim questioned her. "When you came downstairs this morning, was the door locked or unlocked?"

Marissa searched her brain for specific memories, but found none. "I don't know," she said. "I don't remember. I opened the door when I saw you coming, but I can't remember if I unlocked it or not."

The fact that she couldn't remember something so simple brought tears spilling down her cheeks.

"It's okay," Asim consoled her. "You've been through a lot."

She thought she might get a hug out of him, but he took off toward the stairs, asking, "Is it okay if I go up here?"

"Sure," she said, feeling slightly stunned.

"I just want to make absolutely sure no one's hanging around."

"Be careful," she warned, following a few paces behind him.

He stopped when he reached the upstairs hallway. "This is the tinsel?"

She peeked around his muscled shoulder. Seeing that small bit of silver on the floor made her stomach clench. She felt dizzy and grabbed hold of Asim's arm.

Glancing back at her, he asked, "Can I pick it up?"

She nodded, and he leaned in to examine it. When he looked up toward the ceiling, Marissa said, "That's the attic access. You pull that cord and a little set of stairs comes down."

"Can I go up there?" he asked.

She nodded again.

Asim shoved the shard of tinsel in the pocket of his track pants, maybe to get it out of sight. Anyone could see how it upset Marissa. Must seem silly, to him—being upset by a strand of tinsel—but if it did, he didn't let on. He was a better man than most.

He grabbed the large wooden bead at the end of the rope hanging from the attic access and pulled. The rickety set of stairs glided down without remark.

"Wow," Asim said. "It's quiet. I was expecting a squeal or a squeak or something."

"No," Marissa replied. "Nick is right on top of that stuff. He takes good care of me, and the house."

"Oil can," Asim replied, imitating the Tin Man from The Wizard of Oz.

When Marissa didn't laugh, he let out a nervous chuckle, then started up the attic stairs.

"Be careful," Marissa warned as she held the ladder-like staircase steady.

"Don't worry, Riss. If anyone's up here, I can take him."

She'd just meant that he ought to be cautious on the ladder, and not bump his head on the access surround. She knew there was nobody up there. She wasn't convinced anyone had been up there to begin with.

It was strange to see such a large man rising up into that small entry point. The image made her heart race.

"Hello?" Asim called when he had half his body in the attic. "Anybody here?"

Marissa's heart locked as she listened for an answer.

None came, of course. Only the piercing silence of a lonely home.

Asim continued up the ladder while Marissa watched from below. She felt as though Asim were suddenly more worked up than she, which was hard to imagine, but she felt strangely calm, which was also hard to imagine. Sometimes what she took for calm could more accurately be called numbness, but whatever it was, it was better than going out of her mind with anxiety.

"What do you see?" she asked after a moment.

When no response came, she scurried up the ladder to join him.

Asim turned on the one attic light—a single bulb intended to illuminate quite a large space—and turned around in a circle to take in the sights. They didn't have much stored in this space. No large pieces of furniture covered in dusty drop-cloths like you see in horror movies. Just a bunch of boxes, an old trunk, things that belonged to Nick.

"Does anything look amiss?" Asim asked.

Marissa looked around. Because of the pitch of the roof, the only space to stand was in the centre of the room, but from there she could see all around. She felt strange, dizzy. Her eyes wouldn't focus.

"I don't know if anything's been moved," she answered. "There's dust…"

She couldn't formulate a proper sentence. She didn't even know what she was trying to say.

Asim did. He filled in the blanks, noting, "It looks like the dust has been kicked up over here, around this trunk."

"That belonged to Nick's grandfather. Or grandmother. Or great-aunt, maybe. Someone in his family."

Crouching down low, Asim made his way toward the large black case. "What does he keep in here? Do you know?"

Marissa hesitated before admitting, "No."

It felt shameful to reveal that her husband owned things she wasn't aware of. At the same time, she'd never wanted to know. She'd certainly never asked about the things Nick stored in the attic.

"Can I open it?" Asim asked, resting his hand on the trunk. "Is that okay?"

She turned away before saying, "It's fine. Go ahead."

As much as she trusted Asim, Marissa didn't want him seeing how shamefully frightened she was of what he might discover inside.

When he opened the trunk, there was barely a squeal from its hinges. She only knew the lid was off because of Asim's horrified gasp.

Marissa didn't mean to turn around. She truly did not want to, particularly when Asim warned her, "You shouldn't have to see this, Riss."

But she felt herself turning. The whole room spun, and so did she—twisting just enough that she could witness what Asim had discovered down there.

She could see, now, what her husband had been hiding from her all these years.

7

"**C**hristmas decorations," Asim said, lifting a mint-green garland from the open trunk. "This is old stuff—even I know that. From the sixties, I'm guessing?" When he looked over his shoulder and realized Marissa was gazing down at the holiday ware, his expression fell. "Sorry, Riss. I didn't mean for you to look."

She fought the flashbacks every way she knew how. There were probably better and more effective ways than numbing out, but that's what she had to do sometimes. Leave her body. See the room from outside herself. Wave goodbye to the trunk full of strange mid-century Christmas junk and send her brain out for pizza.

By the time her brain got back, the trunk was closed with all of its contents hidden safely from view. Asim had risen to his feet and was standing in front of her, both hands on her shoulders, asking, "Riss? You okay? Nod for me, if you can."

She tried to nod, but sensed only a slight bounce of her head. Her eyes felt brutally dry, like she hadn't blinked in hundreds of years. She closed them and rubbed, the way she would if she'd just woken up after sleeping until noon.

"Let's get you out of here," Asim said, guiding her toward the trapdoor. "We'll talk downstairs."

She wasn't about to argue, and made her way easily down the ladder. She moved like a spectre toward her safe space, her bed. Asim stood in the doorway, gazing at her from across the room with a tortured look on his face.

"Come in here," she begged him. "I need you to protect me."

She felt like a child. Imagine speaking to a former colleague in such a way, but it worked. He entered her bedroom, albeit reluctantly. He pulled a chair close and sat at her bedside like a kindly doctor treating his patient.

"Riss," Asim said, slowly. "You said you didn't know what was up there in the attic. Who would?"

She pulled the duvet all the way up to her chin. "I don't know. Nick, obviously. It's his stuff."

Asim wouldn't look her in the eye to ask, "Where did you say Nick went?"

"El Salvador. I saw him off at the airport the first day of winter break."

Asim seemed very reluctant to ask, "There's no way your husband could have come home since then?"

"From El Salvador?" Marissa balked. "In the middle of the night? To scavenge around the attic while I'm sleeping? Do you even hear yourself? Do you hear how stupid that sounds?"

Asim straightened in his chair. He didn't look angry, but he did seem surprised. And hurt.

"I'm sorry," Marissa said, begging his forgiveness. "I'm so sorry, Asim. I should never have spoken to you like that. You're helping me so much. You are. Please don't leave. Please don't go."

A weak smile crossed his lips. "I'm not going anywhere. I will see that you're safe. But, in order to do that, I need to figure out what's going on inside this house. None of those other boxes were touched. Someone knew what they were looking for, and knew exactly where to find it. Is there anyone you can think of who'd know what was in that trunk?"

"Well, Nick, obviously—that's why you asked about him."

Asim offered an excusatory nod. "Is there anybody else?"

At first, Marissa couldn't think of anyone. Who had been up there? The movers? The Orkin Man? The guy who checked the attic for dry rot? Who could have known what was in that trunk, much less wanted something from it?

When the realization landed, it struck like a blow.

"Caroline," she said, looking to Asim with alarm. "It must have been her."

"Who is Caroline?" he asked gently.

"Nick's ex. She collects Christmas stuff. It was kind of a thing that came between them—not the reason they divorced, but it didn't help. At Christmastime, she'd go hog wild with the decor, then in January she didn't want to take it down. She'd say she'd get around to it, but August would come and there would still be a dozen nativity scenes set up around the house, and those Christmas villages people have, you know. It was Christmas all year round."

"Yikes."

"I'd have died, if it was me. I could never live that way."

Asim adjusted his position in the chair beside the bed. "Marissa, honey, what makes you think this woman broke into your house?"

She looked him in the eye and knew exactly what he was thinking. "I'm not saying this out of spite or jealousy. I swear I'm not."

"Okay, well..."

"Yes, I admit, I can be spiteful at times and I can also be jealous. I know that about myself, all right? I'm not a perfect person. Nobody is. But I'm not just blaming this woman because she used to be married to my husband. I've got other reasons."

"Good," Asim said, as though he were about to pull out a legal pad and take notes. "What reasons?"

Marissa sat up tall in bed. "When they got divorced, Caroline wanted some items that belonged to Nick—Christmas things, as if she didn't have enough already. He didn't go into detail with me, for obvious reasons, but it must have been the stuff in that trunk. Nick is not a vengeful person. The only reason he'd have kept stuff Caroline wanted is if it meant a great deal to him. You said it looked like those ornaments and things were from the sixties. They must have belonged to his mother or his father, growing up, or maybe that was the decor he remembered from his grandparents' houses when he was a kid. He wouldn't have kept that stuff if it wasn't deeply meaningful to him."

Asim considered what she was saying. "As much as I hate blaming the evil ex for all the world's ills, it sounds like you're on to something, here." He gazed toward the hallway, then glanced down into his lap. "Riss...?"

Her heart slumped. "Oh God, what are you about to ask me now?"

She knew it was going to be something awkward. Sure enough, he asked, "Is your husband still in touch with his ex-wife?"

"No." Marissa's spine straightened. "Why would he be?"

Asim shrugged. "Some people keep in touch, stay friends."

"Nick has lots of friends. He doesn't need that woman. He's got me." Marissa knew full well how haughty she sounded, but she was unable to control her tone. "Anyway, he'd have told me if they were still in contact. Nick tells me everything. We have a good marriage, no secrets between us."

When Asim offered a knowing nod, she could have smacked him. She knew what he figured, but there was no use arguing. Let him think his odious thoughts. Marissa didn't have to take them into her mind.

"There's one way to find out for sure," Asim said. "If Caroline has your husband's stuff, it'll be in her house by now—don't you think?"

Marissa's throat locked. The idea of visiting a home that was decorated to the nines with all the trappings of the holiday season brought her pulse to racing. How could she do it? How could she possibly? Just the thought and she could hardly breathe.

Looking to Asim, she said, "You'll have to go without me.

8

"Go where?" Asim asked, looking innocent as anything.

"To Caroline's place," Marissa answered. "Isn't that what you meant? See if the stolen stuff is at her house?"

Cocking his head, he gave her an odd look. "I just meant we should check this woman's socials. Riss, you are hard*core*! You think I'm gonna break into some woman's house for you?"

Heat rose up Marissa's neck, consuming her cheeks. "No. I..."

"Where's your laptop?" Asim asked. "Can I use it?"

"Sure. It's over there on the dresser. But..."

"If this woman is obsessed with Christmas decor, you just know her house is gonna be all over her socials."

"I guess you're right," Marissa reasoned as Asim rose to grab her computer. "There's your first clue why I take a break from social media this time of year. But who would be stupid enough to post a picture of something she'd stolen?"

Asim shot her a look that said, "Are you for real?" and followed that up by stating, "You give the human race way too much credit, my starry-eyed friend."

Marissa gave a wry laugh, and her stomach answered with a groan.

"Sounds like you could use a bite. Why don't you grab breakfast while I pull up this woman's socials?"

Marissa hesitated. She had trepidations, but she couldn't hope to name them.

On the other hand, her bladder was screaming.

She listed Nick's ex-wife's various handles, silently begging Asim not to ask how she'd come by that information. Marissa certainly hadn't checked in on the woman recently. Not in a year and a half, at least. But in the beginning... well, trust issues.

Asim must have understood, because he didn't ask any questions.

"How will you know what you're looking for?" Marissa asked. "For that matter, how would I know what to look for? I've never seen inside that trunk. I have no idea what was taken. Maybe nothing was."

Staring at the laptop screen, Asim said, "You're right. How do we figure out if she stole something when we don't know what we're looking for?"

"This is hopeless," Marissa groaned, sneaking out Nick's side of the bed.

"I might as well take a look anyway," Asim offered. "Maybe we'll get lucky. Maybe she'll have posted something like: hey, look what I stole from my ex-husband's attic at four in the morning."

Marissa couldn't help laughing. "Well, look, why don't you help yourself to anything in the kitchen while I... you know..." She pointed to the bathroom.

Asim appeared uncharacteristically embarrassed as he popped out of his chair, uttering, "Oh. Sorry. Yeah, I'll just..."

"I've got muffins and croissants in the breadbox. Put on the kettle if you want tea. Nick keeps the ground coffee in the freezer. You'll figure it out."

She was already closing the bathroom door when she heard him say, "Yup! Good! I'll leave you to it!"

He took to the stairs, and the quick creak of descending footsteps reminded her of the sounds she'd heard in the middle of the night: someone scurrying down that staircase, trying to escape without getting caught.

A living person.

Not a ghost.

The only ghosts around here were inside her mind, not inside her house. She wasn't exactly safe, but she wasn't in spiritual danger.

Caroline had broken in to steal Nick's old Christmas ornaments. It had to be her. Who else would do something so petty and weird?

Although she felt bad about taking up so much of Asim's time when he could be at home with his boyfriend, Marissa needed a shower. The warm water soothed her muscles and calmed her mind, to some extent. She felt safe inside the locked bathroom. Nothing could get to her, here.

She took a long shower, and never wanted to get out. But she did, eventually, and dressed in her comfiest yoga pants and a knit sweater that reached almost to her knees.

Marissa hopped down the stairs, feeling oddly buoyant after everything that had happened. She wasn't happy that her husband's ex-wife had broken into her house, but the situation could have been so much worse. This, she could deal with.

Although, how would Caroline have gained entry? There's no way Marissa had left the front door unlocked.

Did Caroline have a key to this house?

How could she?

Why would she?

Marissa was so lost in thought when she entered the kitchen that it took her a moment to process the expression on her friend's face. Asim looked the same way Nick always did when he'd just farted and hoped Marissa wouldn't notice.

"Oh, hey," he said. "You took a shower. That helped, I bet."

Marissa offered a non-committal nod.

Asim was sitting at the round breakfast table in the corner of the kitchen. The empty shell of a muffin liner sat plateless beside Marissa's open laptop, so at least he'd eaten something.

"What did you find out?" Marissa asked, getting the distinct impression Asim had discovered something he wasn't keen on sharing.

He didn't look her in the eye, which only confirmed her suspicion. Then he told her, "Well, there is good news. Or bad news. Depending how you look at it."

Marissa's heart shrunk inside her chest, like it was trying to get as far as it could from her rib cage.

"Do you want me to tell you?" he asked.

She clicked the kettle on. "Sure."

As Marissa gazed out the kitchen window, Asim informed her, "It couldn't have been Caroline. She's skiing in Vermont."

Marissa tried to gauge how she was feeling, but she came up empty. "Vermont?"

"Vermont. She's got a boyfriend she's pretty proud of. Rich guy, looks like."

Guilt. That was the feeling she couldn't pinpoint. She felt guilty for assuming Nick's ex-wife would do something so crazy. Break into a house to steal some Christmas ornaments? Who would do a thing like that?

They still didn't know.

Now they were back to the drawing board.

"There's more," Asim went on. "This is the part I... well, it's hard to..."

"Just tell me," Marissa groaned. She was tired of the runaround already.

Asim appeared hurt by her tone, but he continued nonetheless. "I've been checking out this woman's socials, right? And it looks like she and Nick have kept in touch."

Marissa's heart slammed her ribcage, and then it immediately felt like it was eating itself. "What do you mean they kept in touch? Kept in touch how?"

"On socials. Caroline's got tons of house pics—holiday decor—and Nick's been commenting on them. Publicly. Nothing suggestive, that I've come across. The sort of replies you'd post to your cousin or someone like that. Just thought you'd want to know, since you said you thought they weren't... you know..."

"I know," Marissa growled. "Oh, I know."

Her gaze fell to the glass pitcher, and she imagined herself picking it up and smashing it on the counter—shards flying across the room, glass everywhere, the floor a dangerous terrain.

If Asim hadn't been sitting at the table, she might have lost control. But with him in the room, she kept her emotions in check—barely, but she managed not to break anything.

Marissa breathed roughly through her nose.

It was no wonder Nick didn't tell her things. She got so angry about... well, everything, really. So what if he'd commented on his ex-wife's socials? Asim said it was nothing tawdry, just interacting with her as though she were a relative. That's fair.

Except that he'd never mentioned following Caroline on social media. He never mentioned her new boyfriend or her ski vacation, or her cats or anything related to her. Nick told Marissa about other people he interacted with online. He'd given her the distinct impression Caroline was out of his life forever... when she wasn't.

What else did Marissa not know?

Asim must have noticed, from the blank expression on her face, that Marissa wasn't coping well with this bit of news. He said, "Kettle's boiled."

She offered a pained smile. "Thanks. I'll brew us a pot of cinnamon chai, unless you'd prefer something else."

"No, that sounds good," Asim replied. Every word held more than its weight. He was trying to console her without saying anything related to Nick or Caroline. Strange, but it was working.

"What else did Nick write to his ex?" Marissa asked, trying to sound casual as she poured hot water into the teapot. "Anything about me?"

"Not that I noticed," Asim replied. "But I haven't read back very far. It's not like he's obsessed with her posts or anything, just a comment here and there. I really don't think it's a big deal."

Slamming her hand on the counter, Marissa shouted, "If it wasn't a big deal, why didn't he tell me about it?"

Asim's eyes widened, and Marissa felt hers do the same. Her hands flew to her mouth, as if she could stuff those words back inside. "I'm so sorry," she said, rushing to the table. "I can't believe the way I'm speaking to you."

"It's understandable," he said, calmly. "You're upset. You've had a terrifying night."

"Still, I've got no right to shout at you. You're just trying to help me. And you are helping me! So, thank you for that. Thank you for everything. Honestly. I don't know who else I could have turned to. Aside from Nick, I really don't have anyone in my life."

"What about your ex?" Asim asked. "What was his name?"

"Ted," she said softly. She hoped Asim wouldn't notice that her face was heating up.

"What about Ted? I thought you were still friendly."

"Oh, sure," Marissa said, popping up from her seat to check on the tea. Anything to deliberately busy herself. "I mean, we would be friendly if we were still in contact."

"But you're not?"

"Not anymore."

"Why's that?"

Marissa pulled two mugs from the cupboard and sighed. "Honestly? It wouldn't be fair to Nick. Back when he was still in touch with Caroline—when I was actually aware of it, I should say—I used to get so angry and jealous. And possessive. Nick isn't like that. He's gentle as a lamb. He would never ask me to cut ties with anyone in my life, especially since I don't really have any friends."

"I'm your friend."

She felt comforted by that statement as she brought tea to the table. "You're pretty much the only one," she told him. "Oh, do you want milk?"

"If you're having it."

"Yes, I like my tea milky." She went to the fridge to grab it. "I'm sorry, I just mean I don't make friends easily. I really need to trust someone in order to open up to them. I obviously trust you. But I couldn't keep in contact with my ex after basically telling Nick he couldn't keep in contact with his. That wouldn't be fair."

"So you told Ted all this, and then you cut ties."

"Yes and no," Marissa admitted, bringing her teacup to the table. "I cut ties, yes. But I never told Ted why."

Asim had just brought his tea to his lips when his eyes bugged.

"What?" Marissa asked. "Too hot? Too spicy? It's got a lot of ginger in it, this one. And peppercorns, too."

"No, it's not the tea," Asim told her. "It's what you just said: you cut ties with your ex after being friendly all through the divorce. And you never told him why."

Marissa shrugged. "Yeah. So?"

Asim balked. "So a lot of people wouldn't take that very well."

She shook her head. "You don't know Ted."

"No, I don't. But you do." Closing the laptop lid, he leaned over her computer to ask, "Could your ex-husband have been the one who broke in to your house?"

9

"Ted?" Marissa laughed. "Break in here? No, of course not. He would never do a thing like that."

"Just like Nick would never keep in touch with his ex behind your back."

Marissa's stomach soured. She took a sip of tea to self-soothe.

Asim moved the laptop out of the way and leaned both elbows on the table. "Look, Riss, I'm not trying to upset you. I know you're upset enough already. It's just that, if we don't look at all the possibilities, how will we ever figure out who was in your house last night?"

What a question. It made perfect sense, of course, but Marissa was too insulted to answer. For the first time since he'd arrived, she wanted Asim to go. Leave her in peace. Leave her alone.

Alone?

Okay, maybe not *alone*. Because if he left her alone, who else could she call? Kindly old widow Jones from across the yard? They were barely acquainted.

Apart from Asim, there was no one Marissa knew well enough to call on in times of trouble—aside from family, and she made a concerted effort to keep her distance from that lot.

Especially around the holidays. They weren't horrible people, most of them, but there were too many negative associations.

Even if he'd upset her by suggesting Ted had frightened her in the night, Asim was a bridge she couldn't afford to burn.

When Marissa sipped silently at her tea, Asim followed suit. She knew he hadn't said what he'd said to be cruel, but it was hard not to feel picked on.

After an extended silence, Asim spoke again. "I assume Ted knew about your aversion to Christmas."

Marissa nodded meekly.

"And I assume he knows why you can't handle the holidays."

She nodded again.

"Look, I don't know the guy, but would he have wanted to scare you? Maybe to get back at you for breaking off communication with him so abruptly?"

"He wasn't like that," Marissa pleaded. She set her tea on the table and hugged it with her hands. "You've got to believe me: Ted is a nice guy, just like Nick. I don't marry jerks."

Asim obviously didn't believe her, because he said, "Exes sometimes sour when the relationship ends." He grumbled, "I should know."

"Ted would never try to frighten me." She launched herself from the table to grab a muffin from the bread box. Tearing angrily into the top, she said, "Anyway, he'd have had to know exactly where that trunk was in our attic, if he went straight there. It makes no sense. Unless you think Nick and Ted were somehow in cahoots."

"Well," Asim said, pulling the laptop toward him. "Anything's possible. Should I check out Ted's social media? That would be a start."

"Ted doesn't do social media. He said socializing in real life was about as much as he could handle."

"So I guess he won't be easy to alibi."

Shoving muffin bits angrily into her mouth, Marissa said, "Ted doesn't need an alibi. He hasn't done anything wrong."

Asim raised both hands in the air, as if she were pointing a gun at his head. "Okay, okay! Your ex is innocent. I get it."

"Well, how would you feel if I accused one of your exes of doing something awful to hurt you?"

He gave a morbid laugh. "In that case, you'd probably be right."

All at once, Asim's expression changed. This time, Marissa felt as though she'd offended him, but she wasn't sure what she'd said wrong. She didn't know anything about his past relationships. The only boyfriend she'd met was his current beau, Spence: a kindhearted guy, slim and fit, a good match for Asim, from what she could tell. They'd been together for as long as she'd known him, and she really couldn't picture him with any other guy.

Marissa glanced at her wall calendar, pondering the date. When she was off work, it was harder to keep track. It couldn't be Christmas Eve, could it? She felt instantly flustered, not because the date meant anything in her life, but because she knew Asim celebrated the holidays with Spence.

Standing abruptly, Marissa said, "Asim, I'm so sorry! I've taken up way too much of your time. I should let you get back to Spence."

Without meeting her gaze, he said, "It's okay. I can hang around a little longer."

"But don't you spend Christmas with Spence's family? You must have a million things to do. I'm sorry. I honestly didn't realize until right this second that it's Christmas Eve. Your boyfriend's going to hate me if I make you late for turkey."

"Turkey's not until Christmas Day," Asim said, still staring into his tea. "And Spence isn't my boyfriend anymore."

Marissa thought she must have misheard him, but she played those words over and over in her mind, and they always sounded the same.

"We broke up," Asim went on. "Or, to be more accurate, *he* broke up with *me*. It wasn't my choice and I didn't see it coming, but there you have it: all the dirty laundry you could ever hope to hear."

Marissa slumped back in her seat, then reached for his hand. He pulled it away before she could find the words to express her sympathy and compassion.

"I didn't know," she finally said, though it didn't seem the appropriate sentiment. "When did this happen?"

"First day of winter break," he replied, wavering visibly, as though he wasn't sure whether he wanted to start into this conversation. "I came home from the gym that morning and there he was, bags packed and ready to go. He told me he was heading to his parents and I was like, yeah, no problem. I'll join you Christmas Eve. I thought he just wanted to start the celebrations early. But then he sits me down and says, no, I'm leaving now and I'm not coming back."

Marissa wished Asim would let her take his hand. She'd have been able to express her empathy much better, that way. All she could think to repeat was, "I'm sorry."

He issued a self-deprecatory laugh and went on to say, "I really didn't get it, at first. I thought Spence was talking about Christmas. I thought he wanted to spend more time with his family, that's all. He really had to hit me over the head with it, to finally get the point across. I was stunned."

"You look stunned," Marissa agreed.

Asim raised an eyebrow.

"Sorry," she said.

He shrugged. "Easy come, easy go."

She knew he didn't mean that, but she wasn't prepared to call him on it. This was early days. He was still in the denial stage of the break-up. She went through the same thing, when Ted ended their marriage. She'd been so sure the separation was only temporary. He would come back. He knew how much she needed him. He wouldn't leave her for good.

But he did, and it was hard at first, but she didn't remember that stage of grief so well anymore. It had mostly been replaced by the memory of being easy friends with Ted after the tides settled. She never asked if he was seeing someone else. She didn't want to know. Likewise, Ted never asked whether she'd started dating. They set that topic aside and talked about other things. There was a niceness to it.

Should she give Asim advice, at this stage? Probably not. She didn't even know why they'd broken up. It would be rude to ask. Plus, there was always the possibility they might get back together. Sometimes that happened.

"You know what?" Asim asked. "I'd never celebrated Christmas before I got together with Spence. I'd sort of seen it from afar, on TV and in shop windows, all that sort of thing, but I'd never experienced a family Christmas before we were a couple. That first year, when he brought me home to meet his parents, they really took me in, made me feel like I was part of the household. That was something I'd never experienced."

"Your parents...?" Marissa ventured.

"I've got a good relationship with them," he cut in. "I know—and me, a gay Muslim. But not all Muslims are homophobes."

"Oh, that's not what I meant," Marissa said, feeling stupid and flustered. "I'm sorry. I'm really sorry."

"We get a lot of bad press," he replied before draining the dregs of his teacup.

Marissa wasn't sure how to respond. She was too afraid of putting her foot in it to say much more than, "If you want to talk, I'm here."

"Thanks." He gave her a sad smile. "I've been spilling my guts to my mother since it happened, but it's good to know I've got someone else to talk to."

"You must have friends," Marissa said. "A charming guy like you? You must have all sorts of friends."

His brow went up when she called him charming, but he glossed over the compliment. "All my friends thought Spence and I were doomed from the start: he's white, I'm brown; I'm Muslim, he's not; he's shy, I'm a party animal; he's reserved, I'm a flirt... the list goes on."

"You're a party animal?" Marissa chuckled.

"I used to be, when I was younger. And that's the thing about holding on to friend groups from your teens, or from your twenties: they're stuck with this version of you in their minds, and that's not who you are anymore. That's why it's good to have you as a friend: because we've only known each other as mature adults."

Marissa laughed. She wasn't sure why.

"Look," Asim said, fanning out his hands as if to indicate he was laying all his cards on the table. "Bottom line is this: my house is decorated for a holiday I won't be celebrating this year—or possibly ever again. Everything there reminds me of Spence. I keep staying home, night after night, hoping he'll change his mind and come back to me, but that hasn't happened yet, and I'm starting to think I'm deluding myself. He might never come back at all, except to pick up the rest of his stuff."

Hearing this, Marissa perked up. "You're saying you'd rather not be home for Christmas?"

10

Asim gave an exaggerated shrug. "I'm just thinking, if you're scared to be home alone and I'm trying to get away from Christmas..."

"You should stay here!" she cried. "You're more than welcome. We have a guest room, and I know Nick won't mind. He's not the jealous type. Honestly, he's the nicest guy."

"So I've heard," Asim said with a wink. "I wouldn't ask if I felt I were intruding. It just seems like you might want some company, after the ordeal you've been through."

"Yes!" Marissa said. "Please!"

Getting up from the table, Asim said, "Okay, well, if you're feeling pretty safe in daylight hours, I'm gonna get a workout in at the gym, then pick up a few things from my place. I won't be gone for more than two hours, but if you don't want me to go, then I won't."

"No, that's okay," Marissa replied, her head buzzing. "Go do your workout. Everything'll be fine. If it's not, I'll run out into the street and scream my head off. I'm not afraid while the sun is in the sky."

He gave a good-natured laugh, then said, "One alternative to running out in the street is calling me on my cell. I'll come straight back if you're afraid." As he headed to the front hall, he said, "I know you don't want to hear this, but you can always call the police."

"You're right," she told him. "I don't want to hear this."

While he put on his coat and boots, he reminded her to lock all the doors and check the windows, too. He asked if he could pick up anything for her, but there was nothing she could think of. She would happily cook him dinner tonight. She was glad to have something to look forward to.

"Stay safe," he warned her before placing a wet smack on her forehead. "You're gonna be fine. I'll protect you."

Those words made her heart glow. She felt like she was floating as she waved goodbye.

Why was she so happy about this? About spending the night with a friend who was gay? She shouldn't be so over-the-moon, but her legs were shaking. She felt like her skin was getting zapped with electricity underneath her clothes.

He'd only just left and she couldn't wait for him to return.

11

The knowledge that Asim would soon return had a calming effect on Marissa's system. Eventually. Before she got calm, her insides burbled like a soft drink poured too quickly into a glass. She felt as though her jubilance might escape her, somehow—through her nose or her ears.

She thanked her lucky stars for sending a friend her way.

Too much energy. She needed to do something with her body. Exercise. Yoga. She had old DVDs she used to use. She could put one of those in.

Yes, that's what she'd do. It had been a while.

During the summer, fall, and spring she got moving outdoors. She and Nick went for long walks in town together, and hikes in the woods. During the winter months, they didn't get out as much. School tended to be busy, with report cards and parent meetings. And then, when the break came around, Nick took off to whichever country he was helping out in, and Marissa barely left the house.

Yoga had a calming effect on her system. Just what she needed.

At the end of her practice, she took long, deep breaths and enjoyed lying in corpse pose on the carpet. She never bothered with a mat.

Maybe she shouldn't feel safe in her house, after everything that had happened, but she did. That's the gift Asim had given her: peace of mind.

What would Nick think, if he knew she'd invited another guy to stay the night in their house?

Nick was a good man. He wanted her to feel safe. If that meant having a slumber party with a friend—even a male one—he would understand. He would. Especially if that male friend was gay and going through a rough patch. Nick wouldn't be mad about a thing like that.

As she rested in corpse pose, Marissa heard a faint tap at the front door. Her heart clenched, then thudded, which is what happened every time she heard a knock at the door. Of course, the morning's events had her particularly on edge.

A few seconds went by before Marissa realized it was most likely Asim at the door. He'd probably cut short his workout because he didn't want to leave her alone for too long. That was just the sort of thoughtful thing a guy like Asim would do.

Pulling herself up from the floor after yoga practice was like peeling a very sticky bandage from a very hot sidewalk. She felt glued to the carpet until she was all the way up on her feet. Even then, she felt slightly dizzy.

"Just a second," she called out. "I'm on my way!"

The yoga had taken more out of her than she ever could have predicted. It had never taken so long to walk from the TV to the front door. Maybe it shouldn't have surprised her that no one was there when she arrived, but it did.

Would Asim have taken off just because she didn't answer the door in five seconds flat?

No, of course not.

But he might have wandered around back to see if she was sitting in the kitchen.

Marissa walked on wobbly legs toward the kitchen, and even opened the back door to poke her head outside. The weather was so brisk and the air so bracing she felt it like a slap in the face.

No sign of Asim, but the cold sure woke her from that yoga stupor.

Maybe it hadn't been Asim knocking at the door.

The thought launched new terror through her system. She felt as though her legs might collapse. She held on to the wall for good measure.

As she made her way toward the front door, her heart beat rampantly. It felt like a bomb inside her chest, ticking down the hours of her remaining life.

The sound of her pulse filled her ears until she could hear nothing else.

She peeked around the corner, gazing through the window in the front door. If anyone were standing out there, she'd see him. A person would have to be crouching below the window in order to become invisible.

Marissa's heart hammered as she crept closer.

Who could it be?

What did he want?

When she came close enough to grab the door handle, she inhaled sharply. Everything would be okay. The sun was shining. The sky was blue. The air was cold, but the day was bright. She could handle whatever the world held in store.

Marissa yanked open the door to find a gift basket sitting on her front stoop.

The basket was full of Christmas items.

She started breathing hard, trying to keep control, but failing. The flashbacks came on strong. She tried to shake away the images, the smells, the sensations that accompanied that horrible time in her life, but even after all these years, they bowled her over. She couldn't cope.

Yes she could. Yes, she could. That's what she told herself. She was stronger than her past, stronger than memory. She'd made it this far in life. She could handle this moment.

Her eyes closed of their own volition, but she forced them open. Someone had probably sent this basket for Nick, although who would not have known he'd be in El Salvador? He'd told practically everybody.

Marissa would treat this basket the way she treated the little gifts her students gave her before break. Her kids weren't trying to hurt her. They didn't want her feeling scared and ashamed when they gave her mugs full of candy and white chocolate snowman lollipops. They meant well.

That's what she told herself of whomever had sent this Christmas basket: they meant well.

Marissa bowed to pick it up. That's when she got a good look inside. Not just general gifts for grown-ups, but a little doll and rocking horse toy, other treats to delight a child.

Who would send such a thing? Nick and Marissa had no children.

Who would do this to her?

Before she could slam the door, locking the basket out of sight, her gaze fell to the gift card.

It read: "I can't wait to see you again."

12

"**M**ust be from Nick," Asim said as he looked at the card.

Marissa had called him the second she'd closed the door on that evil parcel. It was still sitting on her front stoop when Asim arrived. She wouldn't allow it in her house. She'd asked Asim to put it in the garage, but he'd brought the card inside with him, thinking the handwriting might look familiar. It didn't.

That could have been anyone's writing. Anyone on the planet.

"Nick would never do a thing like this," Marissa explained.

"Send you presents?"

"Send me *Christmas* presents," she pleaded. "He knows how I am with the holidays. He would never, ever do this to me."

"Just like he would never stay in contact with his ex?"

Marissa's back muscles tightened. "Please don't start that up again. Catty is not a good look on you."

"I'm not being catty—I'm asking hard questions. There's a difference."

"You're supposed to be here to comfort me."

"I thought I was here to *protect* you."

"Same thing!"

"No it isn't."

"To me it is."

She couldn't believe how quickly this had devolved. When he showed up at her door shower-fresh after his trip to the gym, he'd seemed so concerned. She hadn't gone into detail on the phone, just told him someone had been to the door and she didn't know who and she was scared. He'd come to her right away, no questions asked.

Maybe he was having second thoughts about staying with her over Christmas.

Maybe she was having second thoughts about him, too.

Asim's shoulders fell and he said, "Come on, let's have a cup of tea."

"I don't want a cup of tea."

"Sure you do. You always want a cup of tea."

How could she argue? He was right. He knew her that well, at least. She was being contrary for no reason.

No, not for no reason. Because she was upset. Because she was living with post-traumatic stress from events no one should have to endure. She felt under threat and she was taking it out on her friend because he was the only one around.

Asim put the kettle on and opened cupboard doors until he found the tea. "Which one?"

"Cinnamon chai," she replied softly.

She knew she should apologize, but she'd never been good at that sort of thing.

Instead, she said, "There are lemon squares in the fridge. Would you like one? I would."

"Go sit somewhere comfy. Read a book for a while. I'll bring your tea when it's brewed."

She hesitated because she wasn't sure if he was mad at her. "Will you bring me a lemon square, too?"

"I'll bring us both one," he told her. "And then we can talk about this gift basket you received."

13

The tartness of the lemon squares complemented her milky tea nicely. Asim had fixed it just the way she liked. Even Nick had never gotten her tea quite right, but Asim did on the first try.

That had to mean something.

"So," he said, sitting on the chair rather than beside her on the couch. "You heard a knock at the door, you went to see who it was—"

"I figured it must be you," she cut in.

"That makes sense. You were expecting me." The upright way he was sitting, with his legs casually crossed at the knee, reminded Marissa of a therapist. His tone of voice sounded moderately therapist-like, as well. "You looked out front, didn't see anything, looked out back, didn't see anything, looked out front again—"

"I opened the door at that point. That's when I saw the gift basket."

"And you think someone sent it to scare you. Someone who knows what you've been through?"

"It would have to be. Why else would anyone send a gift basket with dolls and toys and children's things? They're saying they know what happened when I was a kid, and they can't wait

65

to see me again. That's got to be a threat, right? What else could it mean? And it sounds like it's coming from..."

She couldn't say who. She hoped Asim would know what she meant without her having to say the words. She figured, by the look on his face, that he did.

"But it couldn't be from him," Asim countered. "Right? Unless he sent it from beyond the grave."

That was true. Marissa had never heard of a ghost sending a gift basket to a living person. Seemed farfetched, to say the least.

But could the jinn do it?

Before she'd worked up the nerve to ask, Asim said, "I'm not convinced this ex of yours isn't behind the weird stuff that's been going on here."

Marissa let out a high-pitched giggle before she could stop herself. "I'm sorry. I'm not laughing at you, Asim, only you never met Ted. He's not that kind of guy."

Asim took a big bite of lemon square and chewed contemplatively. Marissa did the same, only the bite she took was considerably smaller. She felt dainty around him. He was so muscular, so powerful. So masculine. And he smelled good, too.

"Where does this guy live?" Asim asked. "Think I should pay him a visit?"

"No!" Marissa answered. She wasn't sure why the idea made her feel so ill, but she made up an excuse. "He might think I'm sending in my heavy."

Asim cackled. "Your heavy?"

She felt so embarrassed. "I don't want him to feel intimidated, that's all. He might... if he sees you... I mean, with all your muscles..."

Raising an eyebrow, Asim slid his phone from his pocket. "How about calling him instead?"

The idea didn't sit well with Marissa. She knew Ted wasn't behind the gift basket, and she didn't want to rope him into this. It was Christmas Eve, after all. He was probably doing something festive. He always enjoyed the holidays.

"Okay," Marissa relented. "Let me grab my phone."

14

"Marissa!" Ted cheered. "Good to hear from you, Raincloud! It's been a long time."

"Raincloud?" Asim mouthed.

Marissa rolled her eyes. It was the opposite of Sunshine, hence a perfect pet name for her. She wouldn't want word to get out. "Raincloud" was the kind of nickname teachers and staff at school would really glom on to.

"Hi Ted," she said to the speakerphone. She didn't want him getting the wrong idea, so she immediately told him, "I'm here with my friend Asim. We're just wondering..."

No more words came out of her mouth. She knew what she wanted to say, but her body wouldn't let her speak. She floundered, feeling sweat-laden panic rise through her body and dry in her throat.

When she looked pleadingly to Asim, he took the reins and said, "Marissa wanted to thank you for the thoughtful gift you sent."

A woman in the background called out "Who is it, honey?" as a flustered Ted asked, "What gift are you talking about?"

"The gift basket," Asim went on. "Marissa wanted you to know it arrived safely and had the desired effect."

Ted offered a strained chuckle, then said, "Must be from a different Ted. This one got the message when she stopped returning his phone calls."

Asim shot Marissa a look that said, "I told you so."

She had to admit, there was an unfamiliar edge to Ted's voice. He hadn't even spoken to her that way during their divorce. Maybe Asim was right in thinking Ted took it hard when she cut off all communication without telling him why.

"I'm sorry," Marissa blurted.

He said, "Umm... no problem. Hope you track down Mystery Ted."

"Who is it?" the woman in the background asked again.

Ted hesitated before finally saying, *sotto voce*, "It's Marissa and... I didn't catch his name. She got a package, I guess, from someone named Ted and she thought it was me that sent it."

"Did you?" the woman in the background asked.

"No!" Into the phone, Ted said, "Look, I gotta go. Merry—oh, no, you don't celebrate... well, anyway, see you... or... not *see you*. Not in the sense of seeing you." Ted growled to himself, said "gotta go," and hung up the phone.

Asim chuckled privately. He looked like a naughty child when Marissa glared at him from the couch. Clearing his throat, he said, "I think we might have got Ted in trouble with the missus."

"Asim!" Marissa whined, not sure exactly how she felt. "That wasn't fair to Ted. I told you it wasn't him, and now he's in hot water with... whoever."

When Marissa imagined her ex with another woman, a twinge of jealousy worked its way through her veins. That wasn't fair to Ted, either, although how could her secret jealousy affect him now?

"Are you satisfied?" she asked. "It wasn't Ted who sent that basket."

"Well, of course he wouldn't admit to it in front of his lady. Whether he sent it to scare you, threaten you, or even win you back in some ham-fisted way that would never work in a million years, there's no way he's gonna say so when it'll land him in deep doo-doo."

Marissa laughed despite herself. Asim's turns of phrase had that effect.

"For real, though," she said to him. "Do you believe me now? Ted didn't send that thing. I don't know who did, but I'm sure it wasn't Ted."

"Maybe—"

Asim was cut off by a knock at the door.

Could that be the same knock Marissa heard when the gift basket was dropped off earlier? Impossible to be sure, especially now that her heart was hammering in her ears. That internal noise blocked out every other sound in the house, from the hum of the fridge to the buzz of the gas fireplace.

Asim rose swiftly from his chair and strode with confidence across the room, but he couldn't hide the look of alarm on his face.

"Wait!" Marissa cried.

He stopped and looked at her. His mouth was moving, but she couldn't hear anything beyond her own heartbeat. There were times when she had smacked her own head to chastise herself for reacting this way. If she'd been alone in that moment, maybe that's what she'd have done. But, with Asim in the room, she tried a technique that had served her well: she stared into the fireplace and counted down from five.

Gradually, the ambient sounds of her house returned. She could hear the fridge, hear the fire, and hear Asim asking, "Are you okay? You want to stay here while I get the door?"

"No." With newfound assurance, Marissa said, "I'm coming with you."

15

Asim opened the door to a cheery Black woman with a shy child clinging to her leg. Marissa had seen this mother and daughter around the neighbourhood, but knew them only to wave at.

"Sorry to bother you," said the woman at the door. "I'm Florine. This shy girl is Bentley. We live across the street, three doors down." Florine pointed in the direction of her house.

"Oh, yes," Marissa said, cautiously. "I'm Marissa. This is my friend Asim."

Asim nodded gently and said, "Hey."

Florine smiled at each in turn, and then said, "Sorry to interrupt your Christmas Eve, but I think you might have received a package that was meant for me?"

Marissa's heart clenched, and then slowly relaxed. "A gift basket?"

"Yes, that's right," Florine replied. "My husband is overseas and he won't be home for Christmas. He had gifts sent and the delivery company swears they dropped the parcel off. They sent me this picture as proof." Florine pulled out her phone and scrolled to an image of the gift basket sitting on Marissa's stoop. "That's how I figured out what happened: they delivered to the wrong address. I recognized your house in the photo. So here we are!"

"That's Jessica Fletcher-level sleuthing, right there," Marissa replied.

Asim gave her a grim look, but she wasn't trying to be catty, or even funny. She didn't know what she was trying to be.

Sending Florine a genial smile, Asim said, "We've got your gift basket, safe and sound. I'll go grab it for you. Actually, it's pretty heavy. Why don't I bring it to your house? Just give me two minutes, okay?"

"That's very generous." Turning her gaze to Marissa, Florine said, "Sorry about the mix-up."

"It didn't have a name on it," Marissa blurted. "I didn't know it was for you, or who it was for. Or who it was from. It didn't say. On the card. It didn't say."

Florine nodded slowly, as though she wasn't sure whether Marissa was upset with her about the delivery driver's mistake. "Again, I'm very sorry for the mix-up."

"No need for apologies," Asim said as he put on his jacket. "The delivery company made the mistake, not you. Anyway, let's call it a happy accident because, this way, Marissa finally got to meet you and little Bentley. It's good to put a name to a face, isn't it, Riss?"

Marissa swallowed the knot of confused humiliation in her throat. Nodding, she offered a weak smile.

"I'll be over with your gift basket in two minutes, tops," Asim said, waving goodbye to friendly Florine and bashful Bentley.

After he'd closed the door," Marissa asked him, "Why did you send them away like that? Why not just give her the basket?"

"I didn't want her to see that we'd put it in the garage," Asim confessed.

Marissa hadn't thought about that, but he'd probably made the right move. It wouldn't seem like a respectful place to stash what was no doubt a thoughtful assortment of presents from a father and husband serving overseas.

As he slid his feet into his boots, Asim said, "That must be a load off your mind, though."

"Hmm?"

He jerked his head in the direction of the garage. "The gift basket. It wasn't for you after all. Nobody's trying to intimidate you, or scare you or threaten you or anything like that."

"Not with a gift basket," Marissa agreed. "But it doesn't change the fact that someone broke into my house last night."

Could Asim possibly have forgotten why he'd come in the first place? To protect her from possible invasion?

Marissa opened the garage for him, and then headed to the kitchen to grab the card.

"I can't wait to see you again."

Now that she knew the real story behind this message, the sentiment filled her heart with love. An heroic father and husband wanted his family to know how much they meant to him.

As she watched Asim head across the street to deliver the basket to her neighbours, she wondered if the people she knew felt about her the way she now felt about Florine and Bentley: somewhat sad that Marissa must spend Christmas alone, but awed that Nick would willingly forego the holiday season for the betterment of humanity.

She truly admired Nick for the work he was doing.

And yet, as she took the time to reflect on his absent, she felt a gnawing sensation worm its way through her belly.

16

At dinnertime, Asim insisted on helping with meal preparation. Turned out he was an amazing cook. He put on a vintage Madonna playlist, and they danced around the kitchen, belting out tunes Marissa hadn't listened to in years.

Amazing how song lyrics embedded themselves in the memory banks like that.

There were some old memories Marissa would pay good money to get rid of. Not the song lyrics, though. She felt proud that she remembered nearly all the words to *Open Your Heart*.

After eating too much for dinner, Marissa led Asim into the living room and turned off the gas fire. She hated being full and hot at the same time. One or the other was uncomfortable enough, but both together was a wretched experience.

She'd really like to get out of the house for a while, maybe take a walk around the neighbourhood, but she didn't think she could cope with all those Christmas lights. As they walked by people's houses, they'd be able to see in through the windows, to families gathered around Christmas trees, eating gingerbread and drinking hot cocoa, carolling together and enjoying each other's company.

Marissa's stomach twisted. She got so dizzy she thought she might pass out, but she didn't want Asim to know. She didn't want him asking what was wrong. She didn't want to explain.

So she sat on the floor and opened the cabinet at the base of the bookshelf.

"How about a board game?" she asked, since TV and radio were not an option. "We've got Scrabble."

"Hey, hey!" Asim cheered. "That's my jam!"

Turned out he was a master of wordplay. He won by a landslide, then challenged her to a rematch.

"How about Solitaire?"

"What, together?" Marissa laughed.

He shrugged. "Why not?"

"Solitaire is for just one person—it's right there in the name."

With a grin, he said, "It's like being alone together. Makes no sense, but somehow it works."

Marissa grabbed a deck of cards and put away the Scrabble board while Asim shuffled. They'd switched to a moody lofi playlist, and it suited the evening they'd built together.

She knew Asim had only come to protect her from last night's intruder, but she pushed that thought to the back of her mind. She allowed herself to believe Asim would choose to be with her regardless of circumstance. They were having such a good time together. She couldn't remember the last time she'd laughed so much, or felt so comfortable with a man who wasn't her husband.

"Let me know if I'm prying," Asim said as they laid out cards on the coffee table. "But if your first husband was such a nice guy, how come the marriage ended?"

If anyone else had asked her that question, she would have been irritated, but Asim could do no wrong tonight. He'd been great company, the perfect guest, and so she told him, "Marriages can end even if your husband is a nice guy."

"Was the divorce your idea or his?"

Marissa shifted on the carpet, where she was kneeling next to Asim. "I think we've lost this hand. Want to start another?"

"Sure, but you didn't answer my question: who wanted the divorce?"

"It was mutual. We were both ready for a fresh start."

"No way. A break-up is never mutual. There's always someone who wants it more."

Marissa stiffened as she shuffled the deck. "Who wanted it more in your break-up with Spence?"

Asim breathed in sharply, then said, "We're not talking about me right now."

Without another word, Marissa started laying out cards for another hand.

One, two, three, four, five, six, flip.

One, two, three, four, five, flip.

One, two, three, four, flip.

One, two, three, flip.

One, two, flip.

One, flip.

Flip.

Asim picked up the seven of diamonds and set it on the eight of clubs. This hand was ripe for the picking. No need to speak. No sense delving into personal histories.

Except now she worried Asim might think she was the cause of her break-up with Ted. He might fill in the blanks in all kinds of incorrect ways, and she didn't want him thinking things about her that weren't true.

So she said, "Ted wouldn't ask for what he wanted."

Asim waited a long moment before asking, "That's why you broke up?"

Marissa started turning over cards, scanning the coffee table quickly as she replied, "He never asked for things he wanted. How was I supposed to know? He expected me to read his mind, and that's not fair. I said to him: I'm not psychic. If you want something, you have to tell me in words. He said he tried to tell me in other ways—a look, a touch—but I wasn't receptive. I said: *You can't expect me just to know what you want. You have to tell me.* That's when he said: *I want a divorce.*"

Asim placed a Jack on top of a Queen, nodding gently.

"Why don't men just say what they need? Why not tell me instead of keeping it bottled up and then leaving? I never thought that was fair."

"You didn't get a chance to improve the situation?"

Marissa's shoulders fell and she sighed. "I didn't want the chance. It was a relief when he left. I loved him, but I needed more time to myself. We lived in a tiny apartment, and I... I needed my space."

"You've certainly got your space here," Asim said, looking around the house. "And you've got that time to yourself, with Nick out of the country."

Marissa didn't respond. Asim had asked about the divorce, and she'd answered him honestly. There was nothing more to say on the topic.

"Spence said the same thing, about wanting space," Asim told her. He placed a two on a three and said, "Look at that! We're on our way."

Marissa felt his enthusiasm was misplaced—where their game was concerned, and with life in general.

"Every other time a relationship has ended, I saw it coming. Even if I didn't want to admit the end was in sight, when I look back I go: *Oh yeah, things were definitely falling apart.*"

"Maybe you'll feel that way about this one," Marissa suggested. "When you give it a little time, I mean."

Out of nowhere, fire blazed in Asim's eyes.

It burned out just as quickly.

Reminded Marissa of a science experiment she'd watched her teacher perform in high school. She couldn't remember what the substance was, but it went up in flames the moment it touched air. Seemed more like a magic trick than science. That's what she'd thought at the time. But maybe that element, whatever it was, existed in everyone: some sensitive material that blazed as soon as it was seen.

"You're probably right," Asim relented. "I must be in denial. Spence wouldn't have left if we didn't have problems." He cast his gaze upon the fireplace. "Maybe, after the holidays, Spence will tell me exactly what those problems were."

To cheer him up, Marissa said, "Absence makes the heart grow fonder. It's possible Spence will realize what he's missing, with you two spending the holidays apart."

Eyes downcast, Asim said, "Possible. But unlikely. When he left, it seemed... it really seemed..."

When Asim didn't finish his thought, Marissa said, "Things aren't always what they seem."

He didn't reply. Didn't glance at the cards. Just stared straight ahead.

Their game of Solitaire seemed to be over.

Another game was just beginning.

A frisson crossed her skin, as if a ghost were touching her underneath her clothes. She recognized this sensation, though she hadn't really felt it since she started dating Nick. The first blush of love. Intense, even in adulthood.

Marissa felt like a teenager, silly and reckless.

Nick's caring expression flashed across her mind. He was such a good man.

She couldn't think about him now. He didn't deserve what she was about to do. She put him out of her thoughts, pretended he wasn't her husband. Pretended she had no husband.

She gazed longingly at Asim's strong jaw, the whisper of a beard, the wabi-sabi symmetry of a model. His easy good looks drew her closer. She moved toward him, shifting across the few inches of carpet that kept them apart.

When he noticed her approach, he turned. That was all she needed. Tilting her head ever so slightly, she arched toward him. The aim was to press her lips against his. One kiss. A kiss they could build a life on.

One kiss, and then ever so many more. Happily ever after.

But Asim pulled back before a kiss could graze his lips.

Eyes wide with alarm, he said, "Whoa, whoa, no! What do you think you're doing?"

17

Marissa felt as though she'd swallowed cold slime. As the unctuous sensation wormed its way to her belly, she threw out apologies and bolted from the room. Even when she found herself alone in the kitchen, she couldn't stop saying, "I'm sorry! I'm so stupid! I'm married and you're gay!"

It wasn't long before Asim had her in his arms, comforting her by saying, "Hey, hey—it's okay. We're friends, Riss. Just friends. I wouldn't let anything come between us. Would you?"

"No," she replied, her breath hitching with ugly sobs. "You're the only friend I've got, and I go and ruin it by—"

"You haven't ruined anything," he assured her. "We're still friends."

She arched back in a jerky motion. "Even after I tried to kiss you?"

He chuckled warmly, like a dad from an old sitcom. "For sure, Riss. It's understandable. We were sitting in front of that romantic fireplace, playing that romantic game of Solitaire."

Marissa laughed and whacked his chest half-heartedly.

"Remember," he said. "I came here to protect you. I'm not going to bail just because of one little misunderstanding."

"You forgive me?" she begged, whining the words like a child would do.

"There's nothing to forgive. I'll wipe it from my mind." He traced a finger across his forehead and discarded the invisible memory. "There you go. It's gone!"

Marissa felt her stomach starting to unclench, though it happened very slowly and cautiously.

"Tea?" Asim asked.

"Always," she replied, grateful to have someone so understanding in her life. She was lucky. He knew her well. And he'd forgiven... well, if he was going to put that out of his mind, so would she. No use beating herself up about it, or dwelling on something so embarrassing.

Besides all that, she was a married woman. Why would she put her relationship with Nick in danger? If she hurt that man, nobody would side with her. No one on earth. He was off helping the less fortunate while she spent her time locked in her house with another man.

What a silly, stupid person she'd been. Good thing Asim had the sense not to kiss her.

He brewed a pot and set it on the table, then got out mugs and milk. They had everything they needed. Except chocolate. Well, Marissa always had a secret stash she hid from Nick. If he knew where it was, that sweet stuff would be gone in a day.

She didn't like hiding things from her husband, but she wanted the chocolate all to herself.

As she broke off a bit of almond bark, she asked, "Are you going to miss celebrating Christmas this year?"

He looked at her cautiously as she handed over the bark. "I didn't think you'd want to talk about that stuff."

"What stuff?"

"Christmas."

"That's generally true," she admitted. "But sometimes I can distance myself from the idea of it. Like, if we're talking about you and Christmas, I'm not really a part of that situation. So, why not just tell me? If you want to, I mean."

He gave her a dubious look as she sat across from him at the table. Asim had his back to the sliding glass door, which meant Marissa would have had a good view of the yard—had it been light out, that is. The darkness was illuminated only by the windows of the townhouses out back. Most windows were lit up, but not Mrs. Jones's. She was probably at her church, or at a soup kitchen. Marissa could just see the woman smiling gently as she served out heaping portions of mashed potatoes to down-on-their-luck old men.

If only Marissa could be more like Mrs. Jones. She wanted to be a better person. She just... wasn't.

"I already miss Christmas," Asim admitted. "It was such a special time for Spence and his family. And they invited me to be a part of it. They really welcomed me in, never made me feel like an outsider or an observer to their celebrations. From the very first year, his parents bought me presents. Christmas presents! Wrapped and stacked up under the Christmas tree. It was amazing."

Marissa smiled. She genuinely enjoyed her friend's delight.

"Before that, my main beef with Christmas was that it was too commercial, but once I started buying gifts for Spence and his family, I really got into the groove of gift-giving. Especially because I used to make a lot of gifts for them, not just buy stuff. Then it really was from the heart."

"What did you make?" Marissa asked. She couldn't imagine her friend knitting tea cozies or painting macaroni art for his in-laws.

"One year it was a spice rub. One year it was red pepper jelly. I did pickled turnip for them one time."

"Oh, food!" Marissa said with a laugh.

"Yeah, food," he replied, laughing along. "What else would I make?"

"I don't know. When I was a kid, I remember making these bird feeders out of pinecones. Do you know the ones I mean?"

Asim shook his head no.

A smile crossed Marissa's lips as she told him, "You'd slather peanut butter all over a pinecone and then roll it in birdseed. The birdseed would stick to the peanut butter, see? Then you'd tie a loop of yarn at the top so it could hang from a tree. Feed the birds in the winter months. Cute, huh?"

"Very cute," he replied. Then he said something she'd heard from both her current and previous husbands. "That sounds like a nice Christmas memory. I guess they aren't all bad."

No, they weren't all bad. That was true. But she didn't like hearing those words, because they felt dismissive, as if these tiny good memories could compensate for the huge horrible ones.

The huge horrible ones were quick to take over.

Once Marissa's mind landed in that domain, she couldn't breathe. It felt as though ghostly hands had hold of her neck. Something forced the air out of her, like a weight sitting hard upon her chest.

She couldn't take in a full breath. Nowhere close.

Once she realized she was utterly incapable of getting air, she started to panic. As soon as she started to panic, less air could get in.

Asim burst from his seat as this vicious cycle progressed. "Riss! Are you okay."

She shook her head yes, even though she meant no, and he started looking around her kitchen for paper bags. Did she have any? She couldn't think. Her brain wasn't getting enough oxygen at the moment. How could she possibly know anything?

"Okay, here's what we'll do," Asim said. "I'm going to cup my hands across your face. You're going to breathe real slow. Can we do that?"

Marissa nodded, and this time she meant yes.

She felt safe enough with him to close her eyes as he placed his large hands over her mouth. He counted with her, told her when to inhale, told her when to exhale. She did as he asked.

Little by little, she got her breath back. It wasn't a linear process. When he removed his hands from her face she started panicking again, but it didn't last so long this time. They were able to get her breathing calmly a lot faster, with practice.

"I'm sorry if I was the cause of that," he said.

"No, no," she assured him. "You've never done anything to hurt me, only help me. You're a good man, Asim. Nothing that happened to me is your fault, just like nothing that happened to me is my fault. I just can't cope with being reminded of the past. See why I can't be around Christmas stuff? Imagine me trying to walk around a mall with all the elves and Santa and decorations and lights."

"Maybe don't think about that now," Asim suggested, and it sounded like good advice.

"I want to be like other people," Marissa told him. "I'm not choosing to be this way. Some people think I cling to my damage, but it's not my choice. I can't just snap out of it."

"I know you can't," Asim said as he took up his seat at the table. "Would more tea help? What do you think?"

She smiled weakly and took a sip of strong brew. It did help. Tea always helped.

Something so simple...

"I would love to do all that normal stuff," Marissa said. "I would love to be a normal person, but I'm not. I thought I'd come to terms with that, but maybe I haven't. Maybe I wish I could have a normal life."

Asim nodded in silence. He took a sip from his own cup, and then asked, "Have you ever noticed that all the major religions or traditions or whatever you'd call them—they all seem to have a festival of lights this time of year? Christmas is just one, but think about Hanukah and Diwali, Islamic New Year and secular New Year: firelight, candles, fairy lights, fireworks. Seems like every culture found its own way to light up the darkness."

"Holidays seem more relevant, when you look at them that way," Marissa said. "For me, I mean. For normal people, I guess they have relevance already. Family stuff, and... all that."

Asim could probably tell she was going to a dark place, because he said, "We don't need to focus on the family stuff. That's fine for other people, but we don't have to think about it. We can just concentrate on the light."

Perking up, Marissa said, "I just remembered something I used to do when I was a teenager!"

"What's that?" Asim asked, a cautious smile crossing his face.

"Well, I did it for Solstice, because that's the longest night of the year." She got up and started digging through cupboards. "I must have heard about it somewhere, because I don't think I made it up." Bringing candles to the table, she said, "I'd light a candle and keep it going all night to welcome back the sun. My mother is one of those people who focus solely on the bright side of any situation—that's one reason we don't get along: she refuses to admit anything bad ever happens—but she always used to tell me Solstice was the most hopeful day of the year, because the days can only get longer after that."

"Kind of a nice way to look at it," Asim agreed. "Why don't we create our own tradition right now? Christmas doesn't have to be what it was before. It doesn't have to be anybody's tradition but our own. It can be candles and board games and endless pots of tea."

"And vintage Madonna, and all sorts of things," Marissa agreed. "Whatever we decide."

"Because we are in charge of our own lives," Asim added. "No one else but us."

"Exactly!" Marissa raced to the drawer where she kept the matches, but when she got there, dread dropped into her belly. "Wait a second, Asim: what if you and Spence get back together? Then you'll definitely want to spend Christmas with him and his family."

"Riss..."

"And even if you don't, you're such a catch. You'll find another boyfriend in no time. And maybe he'll want to celebrate Christmas with you. And even if he doesn't, he might find it weird if you ask to spend it with someone who's just a friend."

"Riss..."

"Or what if Nick suddenly comes across all those hidden-away jealous bones in his body? What if I tell him about us spending this time together and he doesn't like it?"

"That's not the Nick I know," Asim assured her, rising from the table to set his hands on her shoulders. "Look, Riss, anything could happen in the future. Anything. We can only make plans based on what we know now: you're alone for the holidays, and so am I. Anyway, I'm here because of the break-in last night. I came to protect you. There's no way Nick'll be mad about that."

The break-in. Marissa had nearly forgotten. At the time, she thought she would never get over the fear. Look how long that lasted.

"Thank you for being here," she said, looking Asim in the eye. "You are one of the kindest people I've ever met. I'm so glad you're with me."

"I'm glad too," he replied, bringing her into a friendly hug. "Now, let's light these candles."

They each sparked a match and lit every candle they could. When the countertop and table were glowing with no fewer than a dozen, Marissa turned off the kitchen lights and they gazed at the beauty they'd created.

"Wow," Marissa said. "They give off a lot of warmth!"

Asim held his hands over the flames. "Save some money on your heating bills this way."

"The electric bills too," Marissa agreed, flipping off the light switch and sending the kitchen into warm, comfortable semi-darkness.

Asim took a deep breath, and released a mellow sigh. "There's a lot to be said for candlelight."

"Yeah, it is relaxing. I should light candles more often."

She cast her gaze toward the glass doors that looked out over the backyard. Her eyes adjusted slowly to the new light level, but she didn't mind the pace. Everything slowed once the lights were out. That old familiar scent of candle wax soothed her.

When the kitchen across the way lit up, Marissa said, "Mrs. Jones is back at it." She approached the sliding doors. "The widow who lives over there is kind of my hero. She does all this volunteer work, stuff I really wish I would do. I just never get around to it, you know? You get so busy with school and—"

"Hey, I know that lady!" Asim cut in, seeming oddly excited as he made his way to where Marissa was standing. "I used to pick her up and drive her to her meals on wheels deliveries."

"No kidding!" Marissa said. "That's a weird coincidence, huh?"

Asim shrugged. "I was just filling in for a few weeks in the summer, when her usual driver was on vacation. She is so nice. Like, the nicest, most welcoming, most generous person I've ever met."

Jealousy twinged in Marissa's chest, though she couldn't say why.

While Asim went on praising the woman's many fine attributes, Marissa spied through the kitchen window. Another person stepped into frame. "Looks like she found herself a kindly older gentleman to spend the holidays with."

"Kindly, maybe," Asim replied. "But that guy doesn't look old to me."

Marissa rubbed the sleeve of her sweater across the glass, where it had fogged from her breath. She strained her eyes for a better look, though doing so made her feel like a voyeur.

When she observed the scene more closely, she realized the shirt that man had on looked awfully familiar. She recognized him, even though he was turned away from the window.

She knew that man.

Knew him intimately.

When he turned around, she knew for sure.

Snapping on the outdoor light, she yanked open the sliding door and stepped into the frigid night.

"Nick!" she cried. "What on earth are you doing over there?"

18

Everything felt like a waking nightmare. How could it be real?

How could her husband still be in the country when he was supposed to be three thousand miles away?

Why would he be staying one street over, with Mrs. Jones?

Were they having an affair?

Nick's expression fell when he spotted Marissa across the yard. She could tell when her husband was panicking.

He disappeared from the window. That's when Marissa realized how cold she was, standing outside with no coat or shoes on.

When she leapt into the kitchen, Asim asked, "What happened? What did you see?"

"Nick!" she screamed, as if that were somehow Asim's fault. "I saw Nick over there! He was at Mrs. Jones's house." Grabbing Asim's forearms, she asked, "Why would he be there? What was he doing with her? Asim, what is happening? My world is falling down."

"It's all right, Riss. You'll be fine." He led her, consolingly, to a chair before turning on the kitchen lights and closing the glass door. "I'll go over there. Want me to get him? To bring him back? Then you can ask him every question you want and get answers."

She started nodding before she could speak, and finally found the word, "Yes, yes. Yes, yes."

Asim raced to the front door. Marissa followed. He was already suited up in his winter coat and boots by the time she got there.

"I'll be back in two minutes," he assured her. "Don't open the door to anybody." Taking hold of her hands, he looked at her meaningfully. "Are you okay if I leave? I swear I'll be right back."

"Yes, yes, it's fine," she assured him. "Bring my husband home to me. I need to know what's going on."

She didn't want to let go of his hands, but of course she did. She had to. She watched him from the doorstep as he marched into the night.

When he turned the corner, she stepped back into the house, shivering from the cold. The frigid air was bracing, like a slap in the face. Not that she'd ever been slapped. But she'd read somewhere that slapping someone who was freaking out made them more alert. That's why they did it in old movies.

Slap.

Before she'd managed to shake off the chill that found its way inside her clothing, a tapping noise sounded from somewhere inside the house.

Marissa's stomach dropped.

Could the intruder have been in her home all this time?

Asim had looked all around. Where could the burglar have been hiding? Why hadn't they heard him before now?

Maybe because the sound wasn't coming from inside the house—it was coming from outdoors. The back door, to be exact. Someone was in her backyard, and it definitely wasn't Asim. She'd watched him walk down the street and turn.

19

"Marissa!" a familiar voice called out. "I'm so sorry, honey. I didn't mean for you to find out this way."

It was Nick. In the backyard. He must have hopped the fence.

Relief washed over her as she rushed to the back door. When she saw his face on the other side of the glass, she remembered why she was angry with him.

Pulling open the door, she said, "Would you like to tell me what's going on?"

"I'm sorry," he said, looking around the kitchen. "What's with all the candles?"

"Don't change the subject," she told him as he used the flames to warm his fingers. "You said you were going to El Salvador. I drove you to the airport! Then, for some reason, you're shacked up with Widow Jones? What on earth is happening, Nick? Are you having an affair with that woman?"

"What?" he spat. "Of course not! Why would you think a thing like that?"

"Why wouldn't I? You lied about leaving the country, you lied about your volunteer work, and now I spot you at our neighbour's house? What am I supposed to think? What would *you* think?"

"We're not talking about me right now," Nick replied.

"Oh, yes we are. Who else would we be talking about? You're the one who lied to his wife!"

Marissa wasn't sure if anything she said made sense, but why should she be expected to make sense after the shock she'd had?

"Oh, by the way, we had an intruder here last night," she told her husband. "Probably wouldn't have happened if you'd been home."

Nick's face went instantly ashen. She'd never seen him looking so shocked.

"When I was alone in our bed, someone broke in and got up in the attic. Who was the first person I wanted to call? My husband, of course. But no, you were out of range. No cell service. Email only. I had to phone my friend Asim to come keep me company, as if he had nothing better to do. And all the while, there you were across the yard, keeping secrets."

"I'm sorry," Nick murmured.

"Well, you should be! While you were over there doing whatever it is you do with old lady widows, some stranger was up there digging through your trunk full of old Christmas junk."

All at once, the expressions of guilt and shock on Nick's face added up. She'd defended him when Asim kept asking questions, but now she knew, by the look in his eyes, that her husband was the one who'd scared her half to death. Nothing else made sense. The door hadn't been forced. It didn't need to be—Nick had a key. And who but Nick knew exactly where that trunk was upstairs, not to mention what was in it?

Only Nick had any clue. Even Marissa didn't know.

Every piece fell into place.

Even though she knew it must be true, she still had trouble believing it could be. Nick was a good man. He'd always been a good man.

"Why?" she asked. "Why would you do that? Just to scare me?"

"No," he said, and he seemed serious. "Trust me, Marissa, I would never try to hurt you."

He took hold of her hands, but she snatched them away. "Don't touch me, Nick. Not after you've touched…"

She couldn't finish that thought. The idea made her ill.

At first, Nick seemed perplexed. When he cottoned on, he laughed and said, "What, me and Mrs. Jones? Are you kidding? You honestly think—?"

"I don't know what to think," Marissa cried. Turning away from him, she concentrated on the candles lining the countertop.

"Marissa, come on, now. You know me better than that."

He placed his hands gently on her shoulders, but she slithered away. His touch made her skin crawl.

"I don't know you from Adam," she said, her tone gliding into its iciest regions. "What were you doing with Mrs. Jones? Why would you break into your own house, if not to scare the living daylights out of me?"

Scare the living daylights. Was she becoming her mother? Who else used that expression?

Nick sighed. "Would you sit down with me, Marissa? I'll tell you everything you want to know. You deserve the truth."

"Yes," she said, cautiously easing herself into a chair. "I do."

"Want me to put the kettle on?" Nick asked.

She knew he was trying to comfort her. Maybe that's why she told him, "No more tea. I've had enough."

20

Sitting across from her at the kitchen table, Nick asked, "Can I blow out a few of these candles? It's getting a little toasty in here."

"Too bad," Marissa said. "The candles stay lit."

He tugged at his shirt collar in an exaggerated way, like the Three Stooges.

Marissa found his attempt at comedy highly insulting. She told him so by refusing to reply or react in any way.

When she kept a straight face and said absolutely nothing, Nick told her, "I never meant to hurt you."

"What *did* you mean to do?"

He exhaled so sharply he almost blew out the candles in front of him. "You weren't supposed to find out."

"Oh, that makes everything better!" Marissa cried, throwing her arms in the air.

Nick reached across the table, nearly setting his shirt on fire as it skimmed the flames. "No, wait! I shouldn't have said that."

"You got that right!"

"I only meant..."

"Why aren't you in El Salvador?" Marissa demanded. "Let's start there, shall we?"

"Okay. Yes. Right."

Nick folded his hands the way Marissa remembered doing as a kid, when they would do that "this is the church, this is the steeple" thing.

"I originally planned to go to El Salvador," Nick began. "That wasn't a lie. But, before I dotted the i's on that trip, I got talking with Mrs. Jones. She was telling me about all the volunteer work she had lined up around town, and it sounded nice. Heartwarming stuff. Then she got talking about how it would be her first Christmas alone, now that her husband has passed, and..."

Nick gazed beseechingly at Marissa, as though she would be able to fill in the blanks.

"And what?" she asked. "Nick, I'm not a mind-reader. If you want me to know something, you've got to tell me."

He leaned his head on his steeple-fingers and sighed. "The more we talked about Christmas, the more I missed it. It's been years since I've celebrated in anything close to a traditional way. I just wanted those feelings back, the nostalgic childhood feelings Mrs. Jones brought up in me."

Marissa's stomach twisted. "So Mrs. Jones is, what, some kind of surrogate mother figure for you?"

Nick let out a sound that was something like a groan. "I don't know, Marissa. Why do you have to complicate everything?"

She laughed so abruptly it came out like a bark. "I'm complicating things? You're the one who had me drive you to the airport to catch a flight you weren't on!"

"I'm sorry," he said, matter-of-factly. "I shouldn't have lied to you."

"Then why did you do it?"

"Well, what was I supposed to say? That I wanted to celebrate Christmas for once, but I knew you wouldn't be into it, so could I please spend the holiday with the nice old widow down the street?"

"For starters," Marissa replied.

He looked at her flatly. "We both know how that would have gone over."

"Oh, so your lies are my fault now. Oh, I see. I see."

"Not your *fault*," Nick said. "But be real, Marissa: you do have a jealous streak. If you're wondering why I didn't come right out and tell you what I'd planned, that's the reason. I didn't want you taking out your jealousy on poor Mrs. Jones. She's been through enough already."

Marissa wanted to argue that point with everything in her heart, but she knew she couldn't. She didn't always handle her feelings responsibly, and she did often hurt other people. Not physically. She wasn't violent. But sometimes she said things she couldn't take back. He had her there.

He sounded like a tired child when he told her, "I just wanted to celebrate Christmas again."

If he expected her to melt in that moment, he was expecting too much. "Why did you sneak into our attic when I was sleeping? Do you know how scared I was?"

"I'm sorry," he said with alarm. "I had no idea I would wake you. That's why I came over when I did. I thought you'd have taken a pill. You always do, this time of year. Then you're so far out of it a hurricane wouldn't rouse you."

She didn't admit she'd taken her pill early. Instead, she told him, "Your footsteps overhead sure roused me. I was scared out of my wits. What if I'd called the cops?"

A slight smirk grew across his lips. "I know how much you hate the police."

"So would you," she challenged him. "If you'd been through what I've been through."

His grin evaporated, and he nodded meekly. "I truly am sorry for scaring you, Marissa. That was never my intention."

"So what was your intention? Why did you leave that strand of tinsel outside my bedroom door?"

He looked puzzled for a moment, and then checked the bottom of his boots. A thick bead had jammed itself between the treads, carrying a few ragged strands of tinsel along with it. So the tinsel hadn't been left on her floor deliberately. It hadn't been put there by a ghost or a jinn or even a cat burglar trying to terrorize her.

Feeling oddly deflated, Marissa asked, "What was so important in that trunk up there that you just had to have it?"

Nick gazed at the candles burning between them and uttered, "You wouldn't understand."

"Probably not, but tell me anyway."

He sighed heavily, as if to imply this whole conversation was a big inconvenience. "Just Christmas things I grew up with—decorations that belonged to my grandparents. Nostalgia. Nothing that would mean anything to anyone else, but stuff that meant a whole lot to me."

"Nostalgic Christmas decorations? That was important enough for you to risk scaring me to death when you broke in here?"

Cocking his head, Nick said, "It's not breaking in if I have a key."

Marissa's throat produced a growling noise. She didn't mean for that to happen.

"I don't know how we move beyond this, Nick. You're not the man I thought you were."

He countered by saying, "I'm not a bad person. I just wanted to celebrate Christmas. Is that such a terrible thing?"

She couldn't answer him, because she didn't know the answer. She felt hurt and betrayed, but she had no idea whether her distress was appropriate, much less proportional. Was it okay for a husband to lie to his wife? Did husbands do it all the time? Would this happen regardless of who she married?

Who could she turn to? What happened to Asim? He could talk some sense into her. He was good at that sort of thing.

"Are you okay?" Nick asked. "You're shaking."

"I am?" She looked down at her hands. She couldn't stop trembling. "I am."

She cupped her hands over her face, as Asim had done earlier, and closed her eyes and counted slowly down from five.

When she got to one, the resounding gong of a church bell rang out. She couldn't recall ever hearing that sound before, not from inside her house. Perhaps she was usually asleep at this hour, and the church bell probably rang out only on Christmas Day.

Twelve deep, somber peals, she counted. A ringing procession she felt in her belly, a purifying tone.

Marissa opened her eyes and walked to the window, ignoring Nick. He didn't need to exist right now, or ever again. The choice was hers. No one else could make it.

When she got to the glass door, she looked out across the frozen yard. Mrs. Jones's house was still lit up. None of this was the widow's fault. Nick had probably lied to her, too.

The widow's kitchen window was amply visible in the darkness. Through it, she saw Asim standing alongside the older woman, raising a glass of egg nog and smiling. Marissa's stomach roiled, and she told herself it was only the idea of that horrid egg drink making her sick.

She didn't want to feel jealous. Asim was not her husband, not her anything. A friend, that's all. He was allowed to raise a festive glass to the lonely widow across the yard. He could do what he wanted, do anything he liked. He could spend the rest of his life over there, if that's what he wished.

He'd said they would spend Christmas together, create their own holiday, but she never believed that, did she? Hope was different than belief.

It wasn't an hour ago that Asim had told her, "We can only make plans based on what we know now: you're alone for the holidays, and so am I."

Well, now she wasn't alone. Nick was home.

Asim was not alone, either. He seemed happy to celebrate Christmas with Mrs. Jones.

Everything was different.

Better?

Worse?

Acid filled Marissa's veins as she watched her only friend laugh along with the neighbour lady.

Every mystery had been solved: the break-in, the tinsel, the gift basket, the husband. Wasn't that supposed to give her a sense of resolution? Why did she feel so angry and empty, like nothing could ever be good again?

Turning toward the window, Nick told her, "We can get through this, Marissa. I promise you, we'll be okay."

"Maybe we will," Marissa replied as she stared absently across the snow-covered yard. "Maybe we will, maybe we won't."

You Might Also Enjoy:

Mystic Ridge
A Paranormal Lesbian Novel
By Foxglove Lee

WHEN BEVERLY LANDRY inherits Mystic Ridge, a glorious yet neglected summer resort, she and her girlfriend begin a new life in the small town of Lament. As soon as Bev's girlfriend, Cate, arrives on the ridge, she's plagued by terrifying nightmares involving the death of a beautiful young woman. Everywhere Cate goes, she's followed by black mist and glowing red eyes. When she sleeps, a demonic force guides her toward the ridge. Every day brings a new vision of death.

If they stay in Lament, someone is sure to die.

Will Mystic Ridge tear Cate and Bev apart for good, or will a league of unlikely friends help the couple defeat the evil living on their land?

ABOUT THE
AUTHOR

Foxglove's fiction has been called SPECTACULAR by Rainbow Reviews and UNFORGETTABLE by USA Today.

Foxglove Lee is a former aspiring Broadway Baby who now writes LGBTQ fiction for children, teens and young adults. She tries not to be too theatrical, but her characters often take over. Her debut novel, Tiffany and Tiger's Eye, is set in the 80s and features an evil doll! Other books by Foxglove Lee include: Truth and Other Lies, Sylvie and the Christmas Ghost, Rainbow Crush, Rainbow Elixir, Top Ten Ways to Die, You Can Never Go Home Again, plus children's titles The Secret of Dreamland and Ghost Turkey and the Pioneer Graveyard.

http://foxglovelee.blogspot.com[1]

---

1. http://foxglovelee.blogspot.com/